RICHARD NANAWIN

Buk'was

First edition

This book was professionally typeset on Reedsy.
Find out more at reedsy.com

Throughout my life, I have been fortunate to listen to and learn from many Indigenous Elders, Clan Mothers, and Hereditary Chiefs. This book is dedicated to those who have inspired me along the way.

Basil Ambers, Albert Wilson
Rupert Wilson, William Edenshaw
Susan Abraham, William George
Larry Grant, Dorie Brotchie
John Henderson Sr, Beau Dick

Contents

Foreword

Legends have existed in the folklore of Canada's Indigenous people for hundreds of years. Recent events and tragic endings may have led to first contact with the elusive being of the BC west coast rainforest. Anthropological research carried out in the late 19th century and recent archaeological evidence indicate that the ancestors of the Kwak'waka'wakw people have inhabited Blunden Harbour for approximately 8000 years. Kwak'waka'wakw legends spoke of two forest dwellers, the Wild Woman of the woods Dzu'nuk'wa (Tso'no'kwa), as she is known, a giant, powerful and fearsome figure twice the size of humans. From Northwest Coast Legend, she is a dark and hairy ogress with supernatural powers. Her almost blind eyes are also large and sunken, but sometimes they have a red glow. She is usually portrayed making her wild call ("Uh, huu, uu, uu") with her open mouth and thick, red, puckered lips.

The second is Buk'was, the king of the ghosts; he is a small spirit being whose face looks emaciated like a skeleton but has a long, curving nose. He haunts the forests and tries to bring the living over to the world of the dead. In some myths, Buk'was is the husband of Dzu'nuk'wa. The ancient 'Nakwaxda'xw village of Blunden Harbour is a popular stop for kayakers; its hidden harbour and sandy shore make it a perfect retreat for ocean-weary adventurers.

Blunden Harbour is located on the northwest coast of BC, 16

nautical miles due east by water from the town of Port Hardy on Vancouver Island. The 'Nakwaxda'xw village is only accessible by water and has been inhabited for thousands of years due to its protected Harbour and abundant resources close by. This was a thriving community of several hundred people that were eventually relocated to the townsite of Port Hardy in the summer of 1964; the Village site has never really been abandoned, and the descendants of the 'Nakwaxda'xw people still visit the area for its abundant resources and ceremonial purposes.

Preface

Being an Author and Historian go hand in hand when research-ing a story to write; I lived on north Vancouver Island for a number of years and visited all the locations mentioned in this story. The traditional territory of the Kwakwaka'wakw and 'Nakwaxda'xw peoples is rich in oral history and folklore, I spent many days listening to the oral histories as told by the Clan mothers and Hereditary Chiefs.

Acknowledgments

Writing books is harder than I thought and more rewarding than I could have ever imagined. None of this would have been possible without my best friend, Sherri. You have stood by me during every struggle these last 20 years of successes and failures.

Thanks for being ever present, supportive and non judgmental.

Richard

Prologue

Recent events have inspired me to retell the story of Dr. Clarence Edwards and his subsequent disappearance in 1976 during the archaeological excavation at a site near Blunden Harbour, BC. Dr. Edwards had set out on his own in a northwesterly direction towards Bowman Lake to explore the area for other ancient archaeological sites that he'd been made aware of by the local First Nations people.

Dr. Edwards failed to return as planned. The subsequent search did not indicate he had met his end through foul play or accident. Instead, it appears as if he had vanished without a trace. In the summer of 2016, kayakers discovered the field notes and diary that Dr. Edwards had sealed in a plastic bag. He likely set them adrift in hopes of their eventual discovery. These notes and diary set the foundation for the amazing story I'm about to tell.

This story begins during the last week of August 1976; Dr. Edwards had requested that I accompany him to Julia Island to examine the skeletal remains that appeared to be ancient and possibly those of early, childlike human ancestors. I was a grad student at the University of British Columbia Department of Anthropology during this time. Dr. Edwards was the Associate Dean and one of the founders of the Museum of Anthropology. Dr. Edwards was a very accomplished anthropologist.

He was born in Leicester, England and studied at King's

College. He obtained his Bachelor of Science, attended the London College, and completed a Master of Science before completing his Ph.D. studies at Yale University in 1944. Dr. Edwards joined the University of British Columbia faculty in 1957 and championed the establishment of the Department of Anthropology, as well as the founding of the Museum of Anthropology.

His work in the program took him to many ancient First Nations communities along the British Columbia coast; he was often called upon to examine ancient remains when they were discovered in isolated areas. The following is the story of Dr. Edwards's final weeks and months, his intimate encounters with a new being, not soon to be repeated nor experienced by modern explorers; this is his story…

November 20, 1976

"Here, I am writing my final words as I stand on the edge of an ocean, wondering if my words will find their way back to my friends and family. I can only hope that my journal helps those I have lost understand what has become of me and remember that I never forgot about them. I am hopeful that the tides will draw my journal deep into Johnstone Strait, where it may be eventually found and read. To the finder, you will find many names and stories besides mine in these journals. Please contact any relatives of those mentioned and inform them of their final resting place.

These are the last written words of Dr Clarence Edwards.

I

Part One

1

The Remains

In September 1976, I received a significant phone call from the Royal Canadian Mounted Police (RCMP) stationed on Cormorant Island regarding an extraordinary discovery: a decomposed skeleton had been uncovered on Jula Island, which is located just across from the historic ruins of the Blunden Harbour Indian Village. In addition to this remarkable find, a second skeletal arm bone, which exhibited signs of weathering and age, was also located nearby. The local kayakers, recognizing the importance of their discovery, promptly notified the RCMP. Upon examination by the officers, it was confirmed that the remains belonged to a childlike skeleton characterized by notably small bones and a disfigured skull.

Corporal Mason, the officer present at the scene, informed me that he had captured extensive photographs of the site and promised to dispatch them to my office via the next BC Ferry. Following the conclusion of the call, I proceeded to Dr. Edwards' office to communicate this critical development.

Approximately ten days later, I received a substantial package at the Department of Anthropology containing 60 meticulously taken photographs of the site. Corporal Mason had expertly documented the scene from various angles, effectively capturing the significance of this discovery.

Upon reviewing the provided photographs, it became evident that the skeleton had remained undiscovered for an extended period, with its weathered condition serving as a testament to its age. I expressed gratitude for the recent windstorm that had uprooted a large cedar tree, which fortuitously exposed the skeleton and its accompanying remains. In discussions with Dr. Edwards, he echoed my observations; the remains indeed appeared to be childlike yet significantly smaller than what is typically associated with human growth patterns. Furthermore, the dimensions of the skull deviated markedly from normative measurements, featuring a pronounced dome shape.

Further examination revealed a significant depression, likely resulting from blunt force trauma, situated behind the left ear and nestled between the right temporal and occipital sutures of the skull. A closer inspection of the photographs indicated that the exposed femur measured approximately 24 centimetres, contrasting sharply with the average adult male femur, which is approximately 48 centimetres. This considerable difference suggests that the individual may have stood between 3 and 5 feet tall and weighed between 25 and 65 pounds. After thoroughly assessing the photographs, I drafted a memo for my anthropology team, instructing them to convene in the Museum of Anthropology boardroom at 9 AM the following morning.

As I departed the university that day, a myriad of questions filled my mind after reviewing the photographs. The shape and dimensions of the skeleton appeared to be unusually distinct, potentially indicating connections to local First Nations communities. Additionally, I recognized that this discovery could attract media speculation characterized by conspiracies and inaccuracies concerning the origins and fate of the remains. Upon arriving home, I promptly scheduled our BC Ferries passage to Nanaimo for the following morning, coordinating travel arrangements for five members of Dr. Edwards' capable field team.

Our team included Dr. Claire Shaw and me, along with graduate students Rob Kinds and Cynthia Giles from the University of Leicester. We were joined by Dr. Sean Smith, a visiting Doctoral Fellow from the University of Munich, who was contributing his expertise to the Department of Anthropology. The next morning, I arrived promptly at the boardroom, photographs in hand, eager to share my findings. I began preparing overhead slides, although I acknowledge that my relationship with technology is often challenging.

Dr. Shaw was the first to arrive and quickly assisted in setting up the overhead projector, ensuring that it functioned effectively. Shortly thereafter, Rob, Cynthia, and Dr. Smith joined the meeting, each bringing their enthusiasm and insights.

I initiated the meeting by outlining the significance of the skeletal remains found approximately 16 miles east of Port Hardy on Jula Island, adjacent to the ancient Nakwaxda'xw village in Blunden Harbour. The recent windstorm had uprooted a substantial cedar tree, which revealed the skeleton hidden beneath. Local kayakers, engaged in a leisurely outing, made this remarkable discovery and promptly alerted the local RCMP.

Dr. Shaw, demonstrating her inquisitiveness, was the first to question the uniqueness of this find, stating, "Kayakers have encountered many skeletal remains in the past. What makes this one exceptional?" At this point, I displayed the first slide, allowing the group a moment to fully absorb the image. Their questions began to emerge, demonstrating their keen interest in the case. Rob quickly inquired, "When do we leave?" while Cynthia and Dr. Smith expressed eagerness to examine the remains.

Dr. Smith concluded our initial inquiries with a pertinent observation: "These remains are ancient, and it appears there are two sets. Will we need to identify them?" I reassured the team that the local police had secured the area and that they were consulting with local Hereditary Chiefs throughout our visit to their traditional territory. For the next hour, our dedicated team meticulously examined the extensive collection of photographs, paying close attention to every detail of this extraordinary find.

2

Jula Island

Upon arrival at Jula Island, RCMP Cpl. Mason walked us through some significant underbrush approximately 500 feet from shore. The skeleton had been found in a shallow depression under the root ball of a recently fallen giant cedar tree. I was introduced to a local Native Elder named Albert; he'd been asked to attend the site to ensure we did not disturb the known 'Nakwaxda'xw grave-sites. We were informed that we could set up our temporary research tent in the clearing, approximately 50 feet from the shallow depression.

I decided to investigate the site for any forensic materials or samples that would be useful in scientific analysis, such as hair, blood, fecal matter, and textiles of any kind. Dr. Edwards had the team set to work by setting up a grid system in and around the site. The local Parks staff and RCMP have cordoned off the area, 250 meters from shore, inland. Our first find was some hair recovered by a Ph.D. student in anthropology. Student Raj Pinder had a large tuft of brown hair that was matted with a dark substance. Throughout the day, more hair was discovered along with what appeared to be a wooden shaft with copper inlay.

We next turned our attention to the extruding bone a short distance away. The bone appeared to be humanoid. The remaining hand bones were scattered around close by. The skull was massive; it had a depressed skull deformation and striations across its breadth. The shape of the pelvic bones indicated the skeleton was male; the thigh bone indicated an approximate height of 4'11". The body was lying in the prone position; the arms and legs were parallel to the body. The bones were extracted one at a time and placed in transport boxes. The ground beneath the body was also extracted for possible evidence of origin.

The skull was gathered up and taken to the research tent for examination. Attempts to extract tissue from one of the original intact teeth would be made aboard the CGV Louis M. Lauzier. Upon examination of the skeletal remains, all the major bones were found to be significantly similar to those of typical human remains. The bony spurs on the bones indicated this individual had a highly active lifestyle and many muscles attached to the bones. I left my Raj and the others to complete the skeletal recovery while I made my way to the CGV Louis M. Lauzier offshore.

Dr. Edwards spent most of the day chatting with the local Elders regarding an ancient village site reported to be near Lee Lake, approximately a 3-day hike across Jula Island. Around 2 pm, a Zodiac from the CGV Louis M. Lauzier could be heard coming into the inlet. It was likely that we were bringing our shore lunch and refreshments for the crew. Dr. Edwards mustered us down to the beach to discuss his plans for a 6-day expedition inland to locate a possible abandoned village. He was confident that the team could complete the rest of the recovery, and he would be back to join us for departure.

Our team spent the evening with Dr. Edwards carefully examining and indexing all the bones, hair, and textiles recovered from the Jula Island site. We concluded our first evening with the firm knowledge that we had retrieved at least one complete skeleton and parts of another, possibly related to the first.

Dr Edwards said he would be getting an early start the next morning. He would pack for at least six full days and look forward to sharing his adventures upon his return. That was the last time I'd ever see Dr Edwards alive.

During the night, as I was restless, though we were firmly anchored on the Leeward side of Robinson Island, the wind and waves of the Johnstone Strait were unceasing in their fury. It was around 6 am when I heard the sound of voices on the aft deck. I could see the First Mate, Dave Johnson, speaking to Dr. Edwards and reminding him to keep track of his time ashore. The CGV Louis M. Lauzier was tasked with other duties; 8 days hence, she could not be delayed. With that, I heard the outboard start and listened to it fade as it made its run for the Jula Island shoreline.

About an hour later, I could smell the morning coffee brewing in a mess, along with the smell of bacon reaching all corners of the ship. It was time to rise and shine. Last night's storm had departed, and the ocean looked like glass against the morning fog that had settled just above the waterline. It was tranquil, except for the distant cry of a loon. I made my way to the mess deck and found Raj, Cynthia, Dr Smith and Claire already making their way through the morning buffet. It was truly a myriad of delicious entrees fit for any seafarer.

Lt. Castle was the ship's cook; he was a jolly sort of fellow from Newfoundland. He'd joined the Coast Guard in 1956 as a ships' mate and decided the galley would be his home. That was 30 years ago. He said he'd prep a shore lunch and set about setting crab traps and sending the boys out to do some jigging on the flats for fresh halibut, but our first of many jigs dinners aboard the CGV Louis M. Lauzier.

While we were having breakfast, we heard a ship's horn. It was the MV Ocean Breeze coming alongside to drop off the 'Nakwaxda'xw Elders, who were to spend the day with us on Jula Island. It would be our chance to learn about some of the area's history and share our findings. Lt. Castle brewed up another pot of coffee for our company; however, they were more interested in touring the Coast Guard's newest ship.

The engine room was first on their list. The CGV Louis M. Lauzier was the latest vessel in the Canadian Coast Guard's west coast fleet. She had an all-aluminum superstructure spanning her 121 feet from stem to stern, with a beam of 20 feet, and cut a narrow line through the water with just 6 feet of draft. Her twin Cummins diesel engines, manufactured in Germany, could muster 500 horsepower and propel the CGV Louis M. Lauzier at a median cruising speed of 12 to 14 knots. She could carry a whole load of fuel, 45,000 litres, a crew of 9, and equipment; she had a cruising range of 1800 nautical miles.

At around 9:30 am, Lt. George called everyone to the rear deck. The 733 Zodiac was ready for launching; we would board it after it was launched and brought alongside. The 733 Zodiac was a capable craft that could accommodate up to 10 passengers in relative comfort and safety for any open-ocean crossing. Visiting Elders Albert and William were both looking forward to the trip ashore, as neither had ever been in a rubber boat.

Our trip to shore was uneventful; however, to our surprise,

we noticed another Zodiac across the bay at Blunden Harbour. It appeared to be a news crew, judging by the large beta camera one of the crew members was carrying and the fuzzy microphone antenna being packed onto their Zodiac.

Our research area had been marked off right down to the beach. We set ashore in a shallow area to make it easier for our guests to navigate the beach and climb to the research tent. We all had to work on conducting a comprehensive survey of our assigned grids. Mine was located right beneath the uprooted base of the elder tree. I pulled out my trowel, pick, and portable screen and began my examination in earnest. Just as I was about to kneel, I noticed a note tagged to a tree in a plastic baggie. It was from Dr. Edwards.

I removed the piece of paper and read the message: "Peter, I left so early that I didn't get a chance to wish you good luck on your excavations. Please don't pressure the team too hard; they'll get the job done. Best, Dr. Edwards." I placed the note in my canvas field bag, truly hoping that Dr. Edwards would find his abandoned village. This was not the first time he had followed a myth to a disappointing ending. Some years ago, he had been told of an ancient village site on Long Lake at the mouth of an unnamed river. We canoed and portaged into Long Lake from Smith's Inlet. After two hard days of travel, we arrived at the rumoured location.

After three days of searching the shoreline and neighbouring inland areas, we discovered a couple of old tins and some glass jars. They were remnants of occupation, but only from the last 50 years or so. I remain hopeful that Dr. Edwards' quest will prove fruitful in the days to come. He is not getting any younger, although he could likely out-hike all of us over challenging terrain if given the opportunity.

As the day went on, we were pleasantly surprised to see Lt. Castle coming ashore with cooking pots and wooden totes. He decided to serve our jig's dinner on Jula Island. He had come prepared; a field kitchen materialized in no time. On a nearby portable table, we could see cabbage, turnips, potatoes, carrots, salmon, halibut, crab, and scallops. It was a feast not soon forgotten by those of us lucky enough to remember that evening. Elder Albert decided the salmon was best barbecued in the 'Nakwaxda'xw tradition, set on stakes and splayed out around the fire until ready. The fish heads were also placed on sharp stakes to be barbecued in the same manner. While the salmon was cooking, Lt. Castle boiled the potatoes and carrots. He would later add crab and halibut, with fist-sized dumplings rounding out our jig's dinner. On a small table to the left, the rest of the meal included mustard pickles, pickled beets, cranberry sauce, butter, and a small cask of Newfoundland black rum.

By this time, the news crew from CHEK TV had joined us. They were welcomed to partake in dinner "off the record"; we would bring them up to date in earnest and conduct interviews the following day. As we all sat down to feast, my thoughts turned to Dr. Edwards and his adventures. Would he find his abandoned village and bring back news of our next assignment to retrace his steps?

We settled down to enjoy our jig's dinner, with the sun setting over the coastal mountains of Vancouver Island in the distance. The coming days would test our resolve and fortitude.

3

Field Notes

In the summer of 2016, I received a call at my office at UBC from Constable Evans from the Alert Bay RCMP Detachment. The Constable said kayakers on the shoreline of Seymour Inlet had recovered a diary containing the field notes of Dr Edwards. He indicated the field notes were found in a nautical dry bag under some driftwood. The daily entries were dated from September 1 to November 1, 2016. The field notes had been reviewed but offered no further clues to Dr Edward's whereabouts and/or demise. They offer some insight into a man slowly descending into madness with an unbelievable tale of salvation at the hands of forest dwellers.

The Constable indicated that the patrol vessel MV Inkster had been dispatched to the area of Seymour Inlet but could not find any trace of Dr. Edwards, nor any further evidence to suggest he had likely been in the area. Cst. Evans stated he would forward the original field notes to my office in the Buchanan building at UBC. I informed Cst. Evans, I was last seen with Dr. Edwards on August 31, 1976, as a graduate student on his final expedition to Jula Island.

A couple of days later, a courier arrived at the 12th-floor reception desk. I was summoned from my office to sign for the package as it looked official. It was addressed to me directly. I returned to my desk, tore open the seal and pulled out a thick manila envelope. I opened the envelope and pulled out 15 pages of handwritten notes by Dr Edwards. It felt strange to see his handwriting again. It had been 40 years since Dr Edwards failed to return as planned to our base camp on Jula Island. I set the papers down, made a cup of coffee, and settled into my armchair to read Dr. Edwards' final field note entries. Strangely, the first page was dated November 15, and it was addressed to me!!

Nov 15th, 1976

If you're reading this, I've succumbed to the wilderness and its wilds. It's November 1, I am standing at the shore of an unknown river. I've decided my end is near, and I hope this reaches you. Please share the contents with my surviving family and members of our Jula Island team. They deserve to know how I spent the last months of my life. Best, Dr Edwards.

The writing had faded over the last 40 years, but his message was clear. I began reading the faded pages one at a time, and his attention to detail was immediately apparent from the first entry. Dr Edwards always wrote his field notes in pencil. He encouraged all his students to do the same. He would chastise anyone who packed around a Bic pen in the field.

Sept 1st, 1976

530am...Up early, clear skies, some fog, grabbed a quick coffee to go, checked my supplies, headed for the zodiac. Landed ashore at approximately 6:30 am, left the research camp on Jula Island, and set out for Seymour Inlet, approximately 10 miles north/northeast of my present position. I followed the old glacier gap to the top of the pass and hiked the remaining 3 miles to the base of the inlet. Set up my second camp, gathered some wood, started a fire, settled down to campfire coffee and some stew that Lt Castle had prepared as a treat. Found some long branches, and the frame is complete. I've stretched a canvas cover over the length, opening to the fire pit. Not the Howard Johnston, but I'll be warm and dry.

Always the practical adventurer and humorist, Dr. Edwards had a sharp wit and could out-pun the best of them. His attention to every detail and his desire to expand knowledge of the precolonial cultures made him immensely popular among his peers at UBC.

Sept 2, 1976 2 am... Morning, cold. The fjord is blissfully quiet. Last night was restless, but the wind picked up, and I may have had a visitor of sorts —the four-legged variety. I found some small paw prints, which looked like a raccoon's. My coordinates Lat: 50.948911 - Long: -127.210007 place me at the western edge of Seymour Inlet, today's destination will be southeasterly towards Lee Lake, Elders had told me I should find a creek on the northeastern edge, there would be two small islands nearby, follow the creek to Lee Lake. 11 am... having a sit-down, tough going, steep terrain, should reach the northern edge of this inlet in a couple of hours...onward... 3 pm... Eyes on two islands in the distance, my destination a bit further, I should reach the same before sundown. 830 pm...reached the creek, set up camp on the shoreline, inlet serene, flat as glass, light mist sitting above the water, sun setting, final hike, and exploration in the am. Lat: 50.973994 – Long: -127.186661

Dr Edwards was never one to complain. His thirst for adventure was legendary within anthropological circles. He was truly the Indiana Jones of his day. Any grad students who joined his expeditions could expect some measure of hardship; however, it was usually gratifying in the end. Some of the Jula team had worried that Dr. Edwards would wander off on his own into the wilderness. I reassured Cynthia and Claire that the fine doctor was likely a bushman in a past life. There was no need to worry. I pulled out a map of the north coast and plotted the line from the original Jula Island camp through the coordinates recorded by Dr Edwards. Much of the terrain where Dr Edwards went missing had been actively logged for years. Forest service roads have even penetrated the remote areas around Lee Lake.

Back in 1976, this area was a virgin rain forest, undisturbed for millennia and managed by the local 'Nakwaxda'xw people for its rich resources. After Dr. Edwards failed to return, a massive search effort was initiated by the local RCMP and Coast Guard personnel. Local Nakwaxda'xw and Gwa'Sala people familiar with the area also joined the search, but to no avail. It is pretty clear that Dr Edwards followed the Elders' advice and followed a known trail to the Lee Lake area. He had a definitive interest in Indigenous oral history and its geographic accuracy.

Sept 3, 19... Tough going; the creek bed was rocky, the water was ice cold and clear, and there were signs of a grizzly. Whole salmon were found on shorelines, missing their stomachs, which suggests a grizzly bear preference for fatty parts. Spotted a coyote a little further up, scampered up the bank, lots of Eagles soaring overhead. 1030am...Lee Lake, at last, set up base camp and collected firewood for the evening. Noon... Walked the shoreline for approximately 2 miles northwesterly, located old felled cedars, with axe marks obvious, and the area cleared for a 30-foot square. The shoreline rocks were scattered, but could be remnants of the fire pit. The old-growth cedars tower over the shoreline, blocking out the sunlight, making precise examination impossible without a flashlight.

2 pm ...The beach was sandy, with some large rocky outcroppings. The area consisted of a small cove with large hemlock branches hanging over an embankment. Ventured back into the tree line and came across the remains of large house planks and posts scattered in an organized fashion. 330pm...enough adventures for today...time to set up new base camp and chow down on some dinner.

Sept 4th, 1976

Up early...rained overnight...lean too held up... stayed dry on my bed of hemlock and spruce boughs. Set up a grid using some sticks and string. The initial area is approximately 80 feet by 80 feet, with the building set back from the shore. The initial assessment reveals a well-placed village site with ample access to waterways, freshwater, and nearby abundant natural resources. Wish the team were here to experience the steadfast resilience of the Nakwaxda'xw ancestors...I am walking on pathways that have been in use for over a thousand years, before white colonial expansion set foot on the West Coast. I walked down the shore for approximately 100 feet, where remnants of depressions along the shoreline were observed. Upon closer examination, some light digging revealed burnt wood and ash at a depth of 2 feet. Further digging was put on hold as I retreated under my lean-to by a torrential west coast downpour...time to stay dry.

Sept 5th, 1976

Fell off a rock ledge going to get fresh water ...possibly broke my ankle...hurts like hell...going to rest awhile...

1130 am ... Crawled back to camp, set ankle with split cedar...tied with cotton rope and elevated.

230pm ... Ankle pain lingering...damn glad I split a fine pile of yellow cedar ... fire is warm... make some tea...time to rest up and figure out how I am going to get back to Blunden Harbour.

4

The Investigation

Reading the field notes brought back a flood of memories of the fateful day our mentor, Dr. Edwards, failed to return to Julia Island. We had expected to see him standing on the shoreline with a story to tell. Since his departure earlier in the week, we had spent our days examining the recovered remains under the watchful eye of Dr. Smith, a friend of Dr. Edwards and a graduate of King's College. Rob and Cynthia spend their time examining the partial remains with Dr Shaw. Dr Smith and I began our investigation of the complete skeleton. Our time aboard CGV Louis M. Lauzier passed quickly as we set to our tasks as assigned. For Rob, Cynthia, and me, this was an excellent opportunity to blend field study with our thesis research projects.

Rob had completed his undergraduate studies at the University of Edinburgh, majoring in history and minoring in anthropology. He had applied to the University of Leicester to conduct his Master's research on ancient Indigenous cultures.

Cynthia was born in BC; her mother was a UVIC Professor when she met Cynthia's father, a British naval officer, and they migrated to the UK. Cynthia grew up near Plymouth in Britain's largest Naval Base, Devonport. She would eventually attend the University of Southampton and graduate with a Bachelor of Science. She enrolled at the University of Leicester and began working on her Master's research in ancient dietary methods. Their research areas would eventually lead them to UBC.

The first skeleton had been removed from the boxes and reassembled on the examination table. The human body has 206 bones; we assembled approximately 129 from the excavation site. Dr Smith led the examination. She set out to determine the gender and approximate age of subject #1. Based on the pelvic placement, she concluded that the subject was likely female, aged between 12 and 17 years old.

Based on her femur length, she was 4 feet 11 inches tall and very muscular for her proportions. Having worked with Dr Smith for the last year, I knew she wanted input in the form of questions from me during forensic examinations. I asked Dr. Smith how she had determined the gender so quickly and approximately the age.

Dr Smith stated that if the lower pelvic region is complete or at least one entire side, the pubic angle will determine the sex of the subject. In this case, the pubic angle is 169 degrees, which, based on graph comparison, is considered a female angle. If the angle were 140 or lower, the subject would be male. The overall shape of the female pelvis is round, whereas the male pelvis is more pear-shaped and narrow. Furthermore, the ischial spines are less prominent in females.

Subject #1 had suffered a high frequency of fractures for a young person, several ribs, the femur, fibulae, spine and skull. Most notably, the fractures healed with little to no sign of infection, suggesting that the injured members of this group were well cared for during times of incapacitation and injury. Dr. Smith indicated that stress during development was most often found in teeth, which record stressors during periods of food scarcity or illness, disrupting normal dental growth. Subject #1's overall dental health appeared normal. The teeth were unremarkable. None were missing, and they did not exhibit signs of dental decay or damage.

Dr Smith began to examine the skull; a significant depression was visible, usually associated with blunt force trauma. It was located behind the left ear between the right temporal and occipital stitch line of the skull. Small pieces of the skull bone were missing from the immediate area of the fracture. However, skull fragments were recovered from the site. Reconstruction techniques matched the trauma area. Interestingly, a high vaulted cranium, narrow orbitals, and, in particular, the prominent, elongated shape, pointed to a descendant of the Quatsino people of western Vancouver Island.

Dr. Smith shared that she'd seen early photographs taken by Frederick Dally circa 1866, the local people in Quatsino had binding or wrapping as a standard to create the desired shape.

Trade, travel and warfare were common amongst Kwak-waka'wakw peoples. How the two young subjects ended up on Jula Island is another mystery. Dr.Smith reminded us that conjecture is not science, rumours do not serve the advancement of science, and guessing is not optional. She had us prepare samples of the hair, dentine, and textiles recovered from the site to be packed for transport to the UBC labs for carbon dating tests.

Dr. Smith estimated the approximate time of internment to be 500 to 800 years, possibly longer. The great Cedar tree that collapsed was over 600 years old. The injury to subject #1 was consistent with blunt force trauma; however, its causation is unknown.

Once Subject #1 was boxed and prepared for transport to the UBC, Subject #2 was carefully unpacked and laid out in the supine position on the examination table. In all, only 79 bones were recovered, mainly from the upper torso, including the lower jaw, cervical vertebrae, and ribs. One single fibula was recovered. Shallow burials covered in wooden boxes were common practice; the scattering of the remains was often a result of local animals foraging. Dr. Smith began her examination with the lower jaw; the teeth were unremarkable and in a healthy state. Something caught Dr. Smith's attention: of the nine rib bones that were recovered, two showed malformations consistent with osteoporosis or advanced bone degeneration. Dr. Smith commented that she had seen the condition while researching rare bone diseases, the most likely being a rare vanishing bone disease, also known as Vanishing Bone disease. She stated that the disease was sporadic; it had been first described in 1838 by Dr.Jackson. It was further investigated and published in a Medical Journal by Dr. Orham Stout in 1955. To date, there is no cure; the malignant nature and destructive progression limit any positive outcome for the patient.

Dr. Smith returned to the lower jaw and took precise measurements related to mandibular length. Dr Cynthia Giles joined the conversation and stated that the mandibular length could be used to determine sex in the absence of the pelvis or cranial bones. She went on to state that the mandibular length is around 0.544 cm versus.255 cm in females; in this instance, the measurement was recorded at 7.21 cm; subject #2 was female.

5

The Search

After reading the first few entries made by Dr. Edwards, memories of that fateful adventure so many years ago came flooding back. Reading the final note left by Dr. Edwards, hearing the Zodiac engine roar away, I didn't know it was the last time I'd see my mentor and friend. Our research trip had turned into an all-out search for any clues to Dr. Edwards's disappearance. Days turned into weeks, but to no avail. We'd started our journey the last week in August 1976, arriving on Jula Island on a Sunday morning; it was August 29th, 1976. Our research team's nature led to many discussions about the 1976 Olympics, held in Montreal earlier that summer. The entire Royal Family had attended. Bruce Jenner had won the decathlon, and Nadia Comaneci scored all 10's in gymnastics. Dr. Edwards had departed on Monday; he was up early and hadn't said goodbye to anyone except Lt. George, who had taken him ashore in the Zodiac.

We'd followed up with our examinations as directed by Dr. Smith; the specimens had been packed for transport. We had expected Dr. Edwards to reappear sometime Saturday morning or late afternoon with grand tales of his forest adventure. On Saturday morning, Lt. Castle had prepared our usual breakfast fare: bacon, ham, and sausages, accompanied by sides of pancakes, hash browns, and toast. We were all looking forward to heading home and getting back into our beds. Not to say the CGV Louis M. Lauzier did not have all the comforts of home, however, I looked forward to my bed not rocking whilst I tried to sleep each night.

While we were eating brunch, Captain Murray said we'd get underway shortly after Dr. Edwards arrived. The Zodiac was secured on deck. He reminded us to stow our gear for the return journey. A midsummer storm was headed our way down Johnstone Strait. It might get a little rough. Saturday afternoon came and went, the wind was picking up, and Captain Murray pointed the bow of CGV Louis M. Lauzier into the wind to ease the ship's rocking. My research partners were relieved not to be sickened by rocking.

At the ship's bell rang four bells, Captain Murray made his concerns known. He was due back in Port Hardy for fuel and supplies. There was no sign of Dr. Edwards on the shoreline. You could see a small fire on the distant shoreline. Lt Castle had gone ashore and was waiting for Dr. Edwards at the abandoned research camp. As the ship's bell rang 6, Lt Castle could be heard over the ship's hailing system calling everyone for dinner. His voice echoed across the water of the inlet. I could listen to the Zodiac approaching, hoping Dr. Edwards would join us for dinner.

As the Zodiac pulled along, it was apparent that Lt. George was by himself. He'd heard the call for dinner and decided to join us for something to eat. He said he'd head back after dinner. He invited us to join him to wait for Dr Edwards. Dr Smith and

I decided to take up his offer. Lt Castle had outdone himself. He'd been out earlier jigging for halibut. He was very successful, and we all benefited from his expertise in fishing. After an hour of eating and chatting, Lt George, Dr Smith and I finally made our way back to the Zodiac. While we were inbound, we could hear the ship's bell ring 8 times.

The weather was getting rough going in, but joyfully calm once we entered the inlet. Smoke hung over the inlet from the smouldering fire pit. We pulled ashore and made our way to the old research camp. I looked in the direction Dr Edwards said he'd be heading; a low shadow hung over the cedar trees as the sun was setting behind us. Dr. Smith has brought a thermos of hot chocolate and some Nanaimo bars she'd packed along for a dessert snack while we waited patiently.

I decided to take a short walk down the shoreline and walk into the tree line. Cedars of all sizes surrounded me, and the canopy was well over 100 feet above my head. Once you left the shoreline, the canopy made it even darker than it was. I could see the sunset and the reflection off the water.

I knew Dr Edwards was an experienced mountaineer and hiker; I'd joined him some years ago when we ventured into the Stikine area of BC to Mount Edziza. It was the location of BC's largest Obsidian deposit. We'd hiked in from Telegraph Creek, following the old Tahltan trail to Mt. Edziza Plateau and volcanic ridge —a very arduous journey but a most inspiring adventure. I returned to the camp and warmed up by the fire, and we waited patiently for Dr. Edwards to emerge from the forest as the sky darkened.

We stayed ashore until 11 pm Lt. Castle said the weather was moving in, and we should head back to the ship. We would return to shore in the morning. We climbed aboard the Zodiac and made our way towards the exit of the inlet. The tide was changing, and the current was working against us.

Lt. Castle pushed the throttle, and we forged ahead through the passage onto open water. We could see the CGV Louis M. Lauzier in the distance; she shone like a beacon with all her deck lights ablaze. We headed straight for her starboard side. When we arrived, we jumped on the steps and made our way inside to escape the rain.

The rest of the team was assembled in the mess hall; they appeared anxious and wanted an update on the whereabouts of Dr. Edwards. I have nothing to say except that he hadn't returned as planned; we'd go back ashore in the morning. Everyone retired to their bunks for the night, as a restless night would overtake most everyone, hoping for Dr. Edwards' return.

6

Missing

The ship's bell awoke me at 6 am, and Lt. Castle was hard at work cooking our morning breakfast. I was hopeful that Dr. Edwards would be standing on the shoreline, waving to us as we came in. Like the rest of the team, we had grown accustomed to the ship's routine. I knew that breakfast was served at seven bells. Captain Murray joined us for breakfast and was looking forward to going ashore himself, hopefully to greet Dr. Edwards upon his expected return. Lt. Castle had decided to make some biscuits and gravy to accompany our bacon, eggs, and hash browns.

He made the most amazing seafarers' coffee. He would use a heavy, thick-bottomed pot and bring a gallon of water to a boil. He would pour in Edwards' ground coffee by hand and stir slowly while bringing it to a slow rolling boil, then add Rogers' sugar and continue to boil. Finally, he would add Pacific condensed milk and turn the heat down to low. He would let it simmer and pour it into the large coffee pots for each table. After we'd had a fair share of breakfast, the ship's Boatswain's whistle would sound for the "away boats" signal. This meant the Zodiac was preparing to go ashore. We'd learned that the Boatswain whistle also sounded each time the Captain addressed his crew, just like on Star Trek.

It was 8:30 am when we pushed away from the ship. Captain Murray, Dr. Smith, and I started our trip towards the bay. The narrow passage can be rough at times, depending on the tide; the opening is no wider than 40 feet, with overhanging rocks. Once through the passage, the bay opens up with Jula Island to the right and the abandoned Nakwaxda'xw village of Ba'as. As we approached the shoreline, there was no sign of Dr. Edwards. We put ashore and set out on foot towards the forest edge, and we all began calling out for Dr. Edwards. We spent the next couple of hours walking the shoreline calling out his name, but to no avail. Captain Murray reminded us that he was due back in Port Hardy this evening for crew change, fuel and supplies. He could not keep his ship on station for another evening; he must return to Port Hardy.

We decided it best to take Captain Murray's advice and depart for the ship. Captain Murray left his portable marine radio and battery at the base of the reef at our former campsite. Edwards emerged; he would have a way to contact the Coast Guard for assistance and rescue. We boarded the Zodiac and made our way back to the ship. It was a quiet trip back; no one said a word. After we boarded, Dr Smith assembled the research team in the mess hall and delivered the bad news. Since Dr. Edwards has not returned, she would assume a Supervisory role on behalf of the University. She was very hopeful Dr Edwards would materialize in the coming days, and we could put this misadventure behind us. Captain Murray joined us in the mess hall. He said he'd called Port Hardy via radio telephone and had made reservations for us at the Sea Gate Hotel.

Captain Murray stated that he would submit his deployment report and initiate the process of tasking the CGV Louis M. Lauzier for a search and rescue deployment. Dr. Smith had arranged for the team to fly back to Vancouver via Pacific Western Airlines from Port Hardy Airport. I was tasked with staying behind with Dr Smith to assist with search efforts, etc. Dr. Smith had already contacted the local RCMP Detachment in Alert Bay and provided the necessary details regarding Dr. Edwards. Dr. Smith had a dinner reservation for the team in the Hotel dining room. We were told to have at least 10 each for dinner, a drink, and a tip.

Once we arrived in the dining room, the mood was less than joyful. One very important person was missing. Dr.Smith lightened the mood by insisting that Dr. Edwards had likely conducted extensive explorations and found something exciting. He would likely have a grand story to tell about his adventures and discoveries upon his return. Our waitress brought the dinner special, which consisted of prime rib, salad, veggies, Yorkshire pudding, and a baked potato. This was to be followed up with a healthy serving of baked Alaska for dessert.

Dr. Shaw, along with Rob and Cynthia, would fly back to Vancouver tomorrow with the recovered remains. The remains would be placed in secure storage at UBC for the time being.. Dr. Smith told the group that she would be meeting with the RCMP and would be making plans to return to Julia Island with Captain Murray and his crew.

7

Buk'was and Food

Sept 6th, 1976

" 730am... Not a great morning; my ankle hurts like hell, and I can't put any pressure on it. I believe the break is worse than I could have imagined. I should be on my way back to Jula Island by now, but here I sit broken in the bush. Building a fire and making some tea."

Dr Edwards may have thought he was alone, but he was not. A creature known to Kwakwaka'wakw-speaking people of the north coast was keeping him company from a distance. Unknown to Dr Edwards, Buk'was was lingering just out of sight. Buk'was had smelled the smoke from Dr Edwards' fire the first night he'd set up camp on Lee Lake. Buk'was had followed Dr. Edwards through the dense forest, keeping out of sight and waiting for his moment to emerge.

Buk'was was a forest dweller; he is often referred to as the spirit of the dead. He and others live in a realm beyond the sight of man, haunted by those poor souls who have drowned. Buk'was leads those from their human existence to the spirit world. He may contribute to their inevitable fate. Often described as gaunt-looking with a weathered look and bony features. His manner of dress has been described as tattered and torn, his body long and thin with long hair to match. His home is invisible to the living; many other spirits of the drowned congregate near the home of Buk'was.

Buk'was is an early riser; he prefers to wander by himself along the edges of shorelines and forests. If he spots a living person, he will offer them assistance and food. His intentions are not wholesome; he wants humans to eat his ghost food and join the invisible realm. Many a lost and stranded sailor and fisherman have succumbed to Buk'was's offer of food. Buk'was eats his ghost foods from a cockle shell. Any human eating from the same cockle shell will join Buk'was in the next realm.

Sept 6th, 1976

630pm...Managed to build a decent fire. My rations are running low; I only have a couple of days' worth of dehydrated MREs left, so I'll have to make them last. Heard some rustling from the forest edge, likely more visitors looking for a handout. Got my fishing gear, going to try my luck at catching a trout or two for dinner. The sun is setting earlier by the day. I can smell fall in the air, and the morning fog is getting thicker across the lake. Time for some evening fishing."

Dr. Edwards was not an amateur when it came to spending time in the bush; growing up in the Cowichan Valley would have its benefits later on. He was a child born after World War I. His father, John Edwards Sr., was a WWI veteran who moved to Vancouver Island with his war bride, Esther Edwards (nee Montgomery). After serving in the 105th Artillery from 1914 to 1918, he was honourably discharged with a war pension after being injured by enemy artillery in May 1918. During his furloughs, he would spend his time with the other enlisted men at the canteen dance halls in and around Dorset.

It was here that John first met Ester; she was the daughter of William Montgomery, a local magistrate and Major in the local Army Reserve. Married in 1922, John Edwards took advantage of the Veteran Land Act provisions and settled on a small farm in the Cowichan Valley just outside Duncan, BC.

Dr. Edwards was raised in the Cowichan Valley, where it was a rugged existence, with much of his youth spent exploring the local rivers and mountain valleys. He would go on to graduate from Duncan High School in 1944 and return to England to complete his studies at King's College. He obtained his Bachelor of Science degree, attended the London College, and completed a Master of Science before earning his PhD. D studied at Yale University in 1955. Dr Edwards joined the University of British Columbia faculty in 1957. He championed the Department of Anthropology's establishment and, eventually, the Museum of Anthropology's founding.

It was during his time in London that his mate, Anthony, introduced him to military items left over from World War II surplus. During one of their reading breaks, Anthony took the future Dr Edwards along for a hiking adventure in the Scottish Highlands. They traveled by train from London to Edinburgh. It was a long 14-hour trip, but Anthony had booked them a shared twin-bunk sleeper for the journey.

It was during this trip that Dr. Edwards was introduced to military surplus MREs. These would become a staple of many future anthropology adventures. The typical 1950s British Army rations consisted of a canned assortment of meals and accessories for an individual soldier in the field. Anthony reached into his backpack and gave Dr. Edwards a crumpled cardboard box with approximately six tiny green tins. The first contained cigarettes, matches, a can opener, water purification tablets, chewing gum and toilet paper.

The next five tins contained Pork Sausage patties, corned beef hash, crackers and jam, coffee, milk powder, sugar and hard candy.

Sept 7th, 1976

7 am Didn't have any luck fishing, broke out the MRE for an early breakfast. I packed US Vietnam army rations for this trip. Today, I have a choice of an omelet bar (freeze-dried), scrambled eggs and bacon, sausage patties, and cereal with dehydrated milk. I heated some boiling water and added the tins to a slow boil. This would cook the contents and ward off any bacteria that might have hitched a ride. I'm glad I have a bottle of Tylenol, my ankle is almost twice its size and throbs in pain. Time to eat breakfast and figure out a game plan to get out of here.

Buk'was was not far away; he could smell the human food. These smells were unfamiliar, and he wanted to get a closer look. Buk'was waited patiently for Dr Edwards to finish his meal. He usually napped for about an hour after stoking his fire. While Dr Edwards was asleep, Buk'was crept over and stood over the sleeping Dr Edwards. He looked around and saw that the good doctor had not opened the boiled tin of sausage patties. Buk'was reached down and picked up the tin of sausage patties and fled back into the forest. Buk'was found an isolated spot to eat his prize. He'd watched Dr Edwards open the tins with a minor key. Buk'was popped the key from the top of the tin. He inserted the tip and began to twist. The tin opened up completely. Buk'was could smell the human food. He reached his fingers in and scooped out a sausage patty. He opened his mouth and began to feast on the four patties in grease. Once he was done, he dug a shallow hole and buried the leftover tin.

8

Harvison and McClellan

Dr. Smith and I were asked to meet with RCMP Corporal Doug Rowland at the RCMP Sub-Detachment located on Byng Road near the Port Hardy Airport. Since the opening of the Utah Mine in 1971, the population of Port Hardy has grown to over 5000 people. Before 1950, the BC Provincial Police were posted in Alert Bay. They would utilize Police Boats to attend calls for service in the neighbouring villages of Port McNeil and Port Hardy. However, after the dissolution of the BCPP in 1950, the RCMP assumed responsibility for policing in British Columbia. As a result, it was decided that an RCMP Sub-Detachment was required to Police the burgeoning population of the Town of Port Hardy.

We called the local taxi and were met in front of the Seagate Hotel. The taxi ride took about 10 minutes. We were greeted by Corporal Rowland and taken to the interview room, located closest to the front door. Dr. Smith recounted our initial trip in detail, which included the location of our base on Jula Island. We arrived at Jula Island on August 330th. We intended to stay until the following Friday and make our way back to UBC

Vancouver. Unfortunately, D.R. Edwards left for Lee Lake early on September 1. We expect you back by next Friday. After he failed to show up, we stayed the extra night and even left the radio behind.

Corporal Rowland was very concerned; the area where Dr. Edwards went missing was isolated and rugged. He indicated he would initiate a ground search and call in RCMP Marine Services to assist, along with the Canadian Coast Guard. After a visit with Corporal Rowland, we returned to our hotel rooms at the Seagate Hotel to await updates.

Shortly after 11 a.m., Captain Murray received a call from Victoria's Canadian Coast Guard dispatch center. He was deployed to Robertson Island to assist the RCMP with marine and land searches for Dr Edwards. He was informed to be at the station for approximately ten days to provide support. Shortly after Captain Murray was deployed, S/Sgt Rick Ravenhill aboard the Police Patrol Boat 2, Harvison, received a radio dispatch. He rendezvoused with S/Sgt John Silberg aboard the Police Patrol Boat 22 McClellan at Vigilance Point.

They would be coordinating with Captain Murray aboard the CGV Louis M. Lauzier, who would be on station at Roberson Island. S/Sgt Ravenhill and his crew were moored in Bella Coola; they were taking on provisions and extra fuel for the anticipated search and rescue operations. It would take the PB Harvison approximately 16 hours to travel from Bella Coola to Vigilance Point. Meanwhile, S/Sgt John Silberg and PB McClellan were underway northward through the Johnstone Strait. They had just passed Eden Point on their way to Port Neville.

A search and rescue team was en route from Campbell River. The Coast Guard SAR Cutter Grenfell would transport them to the search area. She was currently moored at Kesley Bay, waiting for a fuel and provision delivery. Captain Murray was placed in operational command of the search for Dr Edwards. He had decided that the PB Harvison and her crew would make their way past Vigilance Point and enter Seymour Inlet. Once underway in the Inlet, they would travel eastward towards Harriet Point. Then, they would travel south easterly with favourable tides, make their way to McKinnon Lagoon, and stay on station at coordinates 50.004322 - 127.193570. S/Sgt Ravenhill would coordinate land search efforts by travelling overland to Edwards's last known location on Lee Lake.

S/Sgt Silberg would meet with CGV SAR Grenfell by the Dickson Island entrance and proceed into Morris Inlet. S/Sgt Silberg would sail towards Dove Island IR 12 and establish a SAR station at Creasy Bay. The Campbell SAR team would move on foot toward Lee Lake. Both groups hoped to rendezvous on Lee Lake and further coordinate search efforts. Captain Murray would stay on station at Robertson Island and patrol the Jula Island area daily. First Officer Reginald Sampson informed him that the 442 SAR Squadron from 19th Wing Comox would assist with an air search. In addition, the CH113 Labrador SAR Helicopter would fly over the search grid and report any sighting on the ground.

The next afternoon, S/Sgt Silberg and the Campbell River SAR Team, led by John Hilton, would lead the team overland to the Lee Lake area. Meanwhile, Captain Murray and S/Sgt Ravenhill would approach McKinnon Lagoon ready to disembark to start their overland journey to Lee Lake. Mr.John Hilton was a seasoned SAR member. He'd served in the Korean War with distinction and returned to service with US Forces in the early 1950s in Vietnam. After finally retiring, Mr Hilton became a hunting and fishing guide in the Campbell River area. He'd been raised on a rural property on John Hart Lake, and he'd spent much of his youth in this mountainous region learning the way of the land. When the Campbell River SAR Team was formed, John immediately volunteered without hesitation; his vast knowledge proved to be an invaluable resource for the fledgling SAR Unit.

Before leaving Campbell River, Mr Hilton had made a trip to the local BC Forestry office to view any maps they may have of the area. It was his lucky day; a survey team of timber cruisers had recently surveyed both the ground and air over the proposed logging blocks. The Regional Manager, Jim Blackmore, took Mr. Hilton to the room and found the drawer containing the England Point survey. The map was laid out in a grid pattern; the proposed logging block would encompass approximately 40 square miles, extending northwest from England Point towards Lee Lake. The log load-out and dock systems were to be located on the western shore of Creasy Bay with industrial roads leading inland. Mr. Blackmore provided Mr. Hilton with the coordinates for the waypoints utilized by the timber cruisers; these would be the SAR to the Lee Lake area. The survey notes that the route through the valley was 150 feet above each level, with the surrounding mountains reaching between 1,200 and 1,800 feet. In the elevation, there is a dense coastal rainforest, featuring a mixture of mature red and yellow cedars, fir, and birch. The total overland distance was approximately 8 miles as the crows fly; there are three creeks to traverse and abundant wildlife to be wary of.

9

Old Friends

After reading the first few pages of Dr. Edwards's field notes, it was apparent he was not alone during his last days. He'd broken his ankle badly, and an infection had set in. His notes abruptly ended on September 9th, 1976, and began again on September 19th, 1976. When he starts writing again, he is no longer at Lee Lake. Instead, he'd been moved to the home of a stranger who'd rescued him from certain death.

Sept 8th, 1976

1030am... Not a good start... the ankle had not set well. It looks to have been contaminated and may be developing an infection. I have the beginnings of a fever, and the Tylenol I've been taking is barely taking the edge off the pain. I started a fire to keep warm.

Sept 9th, 1976

745pm...Not doing well at all. My fever is raging, and I threw up my last meal. My vision has been going blurry here and there...my ankle is throbbing. I can see something across the lake between the two Islands, and it is moving toward me. I am hopeful the fever

breaks and I can reset my ankle. Not sure what it is........................
....

I decided to set aside the field notes and contact Dr. Edwards' family. When I met Dr. Edwards at a faculty function, he introduced me to his wife, Patricia. She worked at the Faculty of Medicine, teaching Anatomy and Physiology.

Shortly after joining the Faculty at UBC in 1957, Dr. Edwards met his life partner, Patricia. They began dating and eventually married in 1962. They had three children: Clarence Jr., born in 1965; Jane, born in 1968; and Miles, born in 1970. Dr. Edwards and his wife purchased their first home at 4625 West 3rd Avenue in the Point Grey neighbourhood. After Dr. Edwards's unfortunate disappearance, Mrs. Edwards continues to raise their children in the house and still resides there. Mrs Edwards would eventually remarry in the early 1980s to Dr. Springle. He was also a widower and had a couple of teenagers.

Dr. Edwards-Springle would continue to teach at UBC until her retirement in 2015. Her eldest son, Clarence, graduated from UBC and became a schoolteacher. Her daughter, Janet, participated in the Emily Carr School of Art. She is a well-known West Coast artist. Miles, the youngest, joined the Canadian Navy in 1989. He is currently serving abroad aboard the HMCS Halifax as its First Officer.

Over the years, I stayed in touch with Patricia and the family. Finally, I decided to call her with the news of the Field notes. When I called Patricia, she wasn't home, so I called her cell phone. She answered and said, "I'm at the Robert E Lee Alumni Centre at the moment. Can I meet you at your office around 3:30 or so?". I replied, "That's fine. I'll see you then".

While waiting for Patricia to pop by, I reached out to Dr

Cynthia Giles. She returned to the University of Leicester after completing her PhD at UBC. We'd stayed in touch over the years, but I hadn't spoken to her in recent memory. It was 1 pm at UBC. I decided to call her home phone. It was a little past 9 pm in Leicester, UK. Cynthia answered and was delighted to hear from me. She was saying goodbye to friends who'd come by to play cards. I informed her that kayakers had recovered Dr Edwards's field notes near Seymour Inlet. I now have them at my office at UBC. I read a few of the first passages, including the paragraph addressed to me. "How would he know you'd still be around?" she said. I replied, "Maybe he saw my future and decided I was the best bet. "

We chatted for quite a while and reminisced about our time on the North Island. Cynthia said, "I miss him. Although he was our very own Indiana Jones and mentor, his disappearance always bothered me. It was just like some alien took him off the planet' I replied. "Well, we know he survived for at least three months after he went missing and disappeared altogether."

I replied, "He'd made it to the old village he'd talked about, right across from two islands and a creek nearby. His journal entry described it in detail, including its location, size, layout, and the presence of a house beam. I've read up to his entry on September 9th so far; he managed to break an ankle, it had become infected, he was likely becoming septic, and his vision was failing.

I told Cynthia I would call her in a couple of days, after I had had a chance to read the journal in detail, as it was pretty faded and the pencil-written entries were hard to decipher.

We said our goodbyes, and I decided to visit the UBC archives to search for the 1976 UBC expedition notes. The UBC archives are located in a four-story underground labyrinth of row upon row of boxes. The entire collection is guarded by the UBC gatekeeper, Mrs. Miller. All who enter must pass her strict entrance drill, which includes checking for masks, gloves, and the removal of recording devices. You are allowed a small piece of paper and a golf-sized pencil for making very brief notes. Once you've found the box, Mrs Miller will book you an appointment to view the contents in an environmentally controlled room with CCTV.

Mrs. Miller or her assistant would lay out the contents on a felt-covered table. Any books or notes would be placed in a book caddy; photographs were left in their protective sleeves. White gloves were necessary at all times. Although I was a tenured faculty member and many of the original notes were mine, I had to follow the rules to the letter.

A couple of days later, I received an email from Mrs. Miller stating that my archived records box was ready for review in room three, just outside the collections area. I gathered up my satchel and headed out to the central mall. The archive was located across the mall, a few doors down. Once I arrived, I found the elevator to the lower level and pressed the collections button; the elevator creaked to life, and I slowly descended underground. As I entered the collections area, I was met by Mrs. Miller's assistant, Hanna Young, a graduate student in Cultural Anthropology working her way through her PhD studies. I was escorted to the locker room, where I was to choose a locker, empty my pockets and place everything in a secure locker. After I secured my locker key, Hanna handed me my white gloves, a small piece of paper, and a golf pencil; she then opened the secure door to room three, and there it was.

A cardboard office box sat at the head of the table, laid out before was the contents of Dr Edwards's dreams and misadventure that had come full circle; it lay untouched for some 40-odd years, our original briefing notes, several hundred photographs, receipts, brochures, BC Ferry ticket stubs, and airline ticket stubs. I immediately took the photos in hand; they were all laid out in plastic covers, one by one, and I found my handwriting on the backs of many of them. I'd brought along two of the Faculty's Canon AE-1 35mm cameras, which the Faculty had recently purchased; they came with a Canon 299T Speedlite flash for low-light situations. The University had purchased them from Kerrisdale Camera Ltd. at Old Orchard Mall in Burnaby; I recall being tasked by Dr. Edwards to pick up 20+ rolls of 35mm colour and black-and-white film for a research trip.

The first set of photo sleeves featured pictures of the research team aboard the BC Ferries Queen of Cowichan, departing from Horseshoe Bay in severe weather. There were two pictures included: one taken on the outside deck by a local tourist and another taken inside the main lounge. We were quite a sight, our bell-bottom jeans, white belts, long hair, and dazzling-coloured shirts all soaked by our efforts to get the perfect picture. The next sleeve held a few photos of our arrival in Departure Bay and our eventual boarding of the "Big Blue" Island Shuttle bus.

Big Blue was a monstrous Dodge 15-passenger van painted in a most unattractive blue-tealish colour; I'm not entirely sure how many miles were on Big Blue, but she showed her age. As I looked through the collection of photographs, memories of that fateful trip flooded back, as if it had just happened yesterday. What a motley crew we were, carefree and adventurous to a fault, led by our ever-popular Professor Edwards. The last few sleeves were pictures I'd taken of the rescue effort that was undertaken after Dr Edwards had disappeared. Many of these photos were in black and white; we hadn't used much during the expedition, so I took it upon myself to record the daily events with the film I had left. It was at this moment that I decided to continue the search for Dr. Edwards. I would retrace his steps using modern technology, aided by his very concise field notes.

Since I had the notes, I could make copies and reassemble the original team, but this would prove to be more difficult than I thought. Many of the peers had moved to parts and professions unknown; there would likely be name changes along with obituaries. I asked Cynthia if she was up for an expedition to Jula Island to retrace Dr Edwards's fateful last steps; she immediately said, "Yes, of course, I need a sabbatical and this is how I would like to spend it". She went to inform me that Dr Robert Kinds had passed away doing what he loved best, climbing the world's seven tallest mountain peaks. He would achieve his goal in 1999 but would succumb to pulmonary edema 150 meters short of reaching the summit of K2.

Cynthia recalled running into Dr Sean Smith at a gala event in Munich; he was the Chair of Social and Cultural Anthropology at LMU Munich. Cynthia and I said our goodbyes, and I set out to reunite the dream team.

The next morning, I called LMU Munich and asked to speak with Dr. Sean Smith. Surprisingly, I was connected to his department, and a young lady answered the phone. I stated I was an old colleague of Dr. Smith and would like to speak with him. She briefly placed me on hold and then returned to say Dr. Smith would pick up in a few moments. It wasn't long before I heard, "Is this my old friend Dr Peter Macintosh!!, I replied, "Yes, it surely is!!" I brought Dr. Smith up to date on the recovery of Dr. Edwards's field notes and informed him I wanted him to rejoin the original team and trace Dr. Edwards's trail. Dr. Smith said, " Tell me where you want me and I'll be there.

I look forward to reuniting and seeing British Columbia". I told him I'd plan for a mid-July expedition; we'd meet at the University of British Columbia and take it from there.

10

Buk'was

He could see a man lying on the rocky beach. A small fire smouldered nearby, a half-opened can of food lay nearby, surrounded by buzzing flies. He called out, "Are you okay, several times, but to no avail; he shouted again and again as he got closer, but there was no movement. Buk'was drew his dug-out canoe closer to shore and set it bow on the loose gravel near a fallen cedar tree. As he stepped out of his canoe, he noticed the man's ankle was swollen and infected. Buk'was was likely broken and needed to be replaced. Buk'was knelt beside the man and put his hand near his mouth. He felt a faint breath; he was still alive. He placed his hand on man's shoulder, gently shook the man and called out again, "Are you ok? I'm here to help There was no response, Buk'was located Dr. Edwards' field notebook nearby, Buk'was was not a good reader by sounding out the name on the cover of Dr.Edwards Buk'was was never taught to read, his people relied upon their spoken language; they did not know anything of the pale people and their large canoe Buk'was doused the small fire and gathered up all the belongings Dr. Edwards had brought with him; he gathered any remnants to show no one had ever been at the old village. He threw the bow of his canoe to Dr. Edwards; he tied Edwards together and dragged him towards the canoe. Buk'was was not a tall man, but he possessed great strength. He did manage to roll Dr. Edwards over the edge of the canoe and into the middle; he placed Dr. Edwards's head on the backpack in the back. Buk'was began to paddle his canoe towards the setting sun. Once he reached the end of the lake, he would portage a short distance to open salt water that led to the open ocean. As he approached the western shore, he picked up two rounded branches and began to bang them together in a definite rhythm; tap, tap—— tap———tap, tap———tap; he continued until his canoe drifted ashore. He nudged his short canoe ashore, covered Dr. Edwards with a bear hide, and went to start a small fire. Buk'was gathered up some dead cedar bows and broke them into pieces; he used his axe blade to make some cedar shavings for his fire starter. Once his fire pit was built, he pulled out his flint and began to strike it until sparks caught the cedar on fire. In the distance, he could hear the faint sound of tap, tap—— tap—— tap, tap———————— tap, help was on the way; he had summoned more souls of Buk'was.

As the sunlight dawned, many souls of Buk'was appeared from the fog. They were both young and old, spoke different languages, and all dressed differently. Buk'was seemed to be dishevelled in his torn striped trousers, his filthy white cotton shirt, shredded neck scar, and man's hat. His appearance, voice, and demeanour were those of a British sailor of the 18th century. He told three of them to carry Dr. Edwards through the portage trail, a distance of approximately 2 miles over land through a dense forest. The remaining Buk'was carried the canoe on their shoulders, and a young girl carried Edwards' belongings. Buk'was emerged from the forest; the cold salt air enveloped him, and he was back where he belonged.

He reminisced about his demise those many years ago; his crewmates and his beloved ship, the Pass of Beacon. He had joined the crew at the port of Cartagena, Colombia, and she was bound for timber in Washington State on the west coast. She was a splendid four-masted merchant; she had fine lines and measured 300 feet from stem to stern. She was led by her Captain Harry Scoville, a veteran sailor with a crew of 4 officers and 31 mates. During the first weeks of the voyage, nineteen mates and three officers were stricken with malaria. The Captain remained confident that his remaining officers and crew could bring the ship safely to Port Astoria.

She would meet her demise in the Straight of Juan de Fuca on the rocky shores of western Vancouver Island. Her sister ship, the Pass of Broadmore, had arrived safely in Port Townsend with Captain Olsen at the helm. Both ships had encountered the same storm, a southeastern gale that pushed the stricken Pass of Beacon onto the rocks at Amphitrite Point. Buk'was awoke on the rocky shore and was taken in by a stranger who brought him into the nearby forest; he was nursed back to health, but would never return to his past life; his new life had just begun.

Once all the souls of Buk'was reached the saltwater inlet, they all boarded their canoes and began the journey to the land of Buk'was. It was a hidden inlet, hundreds of nautical miles to the northwest, untouched by time and hidden since time immemorial. After several days of travel, the many canoes entered the inlet, and the many souls of Buk'was began to sing. As they approached the village, smoke could be seen rising from the many big houses along the emerging shoreline. This was Buk'was and the hundreds of souls whose lives ended in tragedy and were resurrected. Once the canoe carrying Dr. Edwards was put ashore, he was taken to a big house in the centre of the village; there, he would be nursed back to health by Buk'was and his many souls.

Dr. Edwards was laid on a great woven cedar mat nearest the fire pit in the middle of the Big House; his clothes were taken and replaced with deer hide coverings and bear hide blankets. Dr. Edwards had fallen into a coma-like state, his broken angle had festered and caused a massive blood-borne infection to rage throughout his body. After a short while, a man with round glasses, a tall, slim build, dressed in clothing generally worn for fall weather in England, emerged from the back of the big house.

He said, " I see we've found another misguided, desperate soul." he replied, "I saw the smoke in the distance and decided to see who had ventured to the ancient village. He needs your medical attention, Doctor." This soul of Buk'was had a name; he was Dr. Franklyn Berens III, the ship's doctor on the HMS Condor, which was lost at sea some 76 years prior. He'd woken up clinging to a fragment of the life raft and was rescued by Buk'was and nursed back to health, so he thought. He'd accepted the help of Buk'was; he was fed food and fresh water, and offered clothes and a warm place to sleep each night. Several weeks later, he realized that something was wrong; he woke one morning without a heartbeat. He realized he appeared alive among the hundreds of other souls, but alas, he was now here to stay, helping lost souls. For eternity, Dr. Berens set Dr. Edwards's broken ankle and reset it properly. He administered some antibiotics from his much-prized medical pouch; he was hopeful that Dr. Edwards would recover.

As days turned into weeks, Dr. Edwards began to exhibit signs of recovery; his infection had receded, and he was no longer feverish. On the morning of the second week, Dr. Edwards opened his eyes and took a deep breath; his vision was blurry, and he could smell smoke. "Where am I?" he thought. "I can smell smoke and hear voices from a distance". A young girl who had been tending to Dr. Edwards ran through the village to find Dr. Berens, who saw him and said," He's woken up, he's woken up".

Dr Beren hurriedly grabbed his overcoat and followed the girl back to the now-stirring Dr. Edwards. He knelt over Dr. Edwards and gently shook his hand, I'm Dr. Berens. You were very sick. I have treated your injury". Dr. Edwards asked for water; his throat was parched, and he was unable to speak. The young girl handed Dr. Berens a wooden mug, and Dr. Edwards lifted his head to take a couple of sips.

Dr. Edwards thought the water was tepid and tasted off, but he took several more sips before lying back down. Dr. Edwards could hear many voices, some Indigenous, others Spanish, French, with some Michif and Chinook. Was he at a trading Port, and how long had he been unconscious? Dr. Edwards took more water from the wooden mug; it smelled awful and had the scent of something rotten. He couldn't resist; he drank until his belly was full. He sat up with the assistance of Dr. Berens and asked again where he was.

Dr. Berens answered," You were found near dead on the lake shore nearby. Buk'was saw the smoke from your fire and found you were unconscious. He and the others brought you to our village, where I treated your broken ankle, brought your fever under control and gave you antibiotics."

Dr. Edward replied, " I am grateful for your help. Where

is this village? I hear many different languages." Dr. Berens replied," You are in Kequesta in Seymour Inlet, it is a fishing village, rest now, we'll speak more later, you need to sleep". Dr. Edwards was thankful he'd been found; he assumed his blurred vision was a result of the infection, and he'd be right as rain in a week or so. Dr. Edwards lay back down and drifted off, thinking about his team, his wife, and his eventual return to Vancouver.

Dr. Berens left the big house and met Buk'was on the wooden pier where he was smoking his pipe. He said, " He's resting, I told him where he was but didn't say anything, he took some water and went back to sleep". Buk'was smiled." Water's a good start, it'll keep his vision from returning, tell the others only to use the first name if they encounter him when he's well enough to leave the house". Over several days, the young girl took food and water to Dr. Edwards. Her name was Mary, and she was one of many souls from Buk'was who had been found after the sinking of the SS Valencia. She had 252 passengers and 22 crew when she struck the rocks off Cape Beale on the west coast of Vancouver Island. Mary was a shy 14-year-old girl.

She'd been rescued by Buk'was and joined the many souls of Buk'was at Kequesta Village. Dr. Edwards began to regain his strength and briefly put weight on his healing ankle. He was helped outside by Mary, who was his constant companion. He asked her where she was from, she replied, " I'm from Astoria, my parents and I were on the ship Valencia going to San Francisco, and our ship hit rocks, Buk'was rescued us and brought us here to recover". Dr. Edwards asked Mary how she'd been at Kequesta, and she replied, " About 60 seasons, maybe more".

Dr. Edwards was taken aback. This can't be right. She didn't sound like she was 70 years old; she sounded like a teenager. Mary gave Dr. Edwards his lunch on a wooden plate, which consisted of a mix of mussels, salmon, and seaweed. It didn't taste good, but it was filling. Dr. Edwards was grateful to be fed. Dr. Edwards asked to walk over to the fire pit near the shoreline. Mary placed a cedar mat on the sand and let Dr. Edwards sit down. While Dr. Edwards was seated alone, Buk'was came by and sat on the sand beside him. "How are you feeling?? said Buk'was.. Dr. Edwards replied," Better, except for my sight, it's still blurry all the time." Buk'was said," Hopefully, over time, your eyesight will return to what it once was.

" How long have I been here? I've lost track of time," said Dr. Edwards. "About three weeks, I'd say you'll be right as rain soon enough, "Buk'was replied. "How did you come to be here, Buk'was? said Dr. Edwards. Buk'was looked out towards the ocean, took a shallow breath and said, " I was a midshipman aboard the Pass of Beacon. We'd left Cartagena, Colombia, bound for Astoria to pick up a load of timber. A couple of weeks into the journey, many of my crewmates developed malaria, some perished, and most were too sick to work. I was lucky; I did not succumb to malaria.

Our Captain decided to sail on with a skeleton crew. Eventually, we saw sea birds and knew we were close to the west coast of Vancouver Island. Later that evening, a gale from the southeast raged for an hour. Our mizzen mast had snapped, and it was dragging astern, causing the rudder to jam. We attempted to cut loose, but it was too late; we ran around on the rocks, which were torn apart and broken in half. I was tossed into the water and woke up later on the rocks.

I was rescued by a local Indian and taken into the nearby forest. I was very badly injured, but he gave me some foul warm tea from a wooden mug, and I fell asleep. I woke here at Kequesta much the same way that you did. My head and eyes had been wrapped with cloth, and I could not see, but I was alive. Over time, I would meet many of the others in the village, and many shared the same story of being rescued. "How long have you been here?" asked Dr. Edwards. Buk'was paused and said, " I'm not sure exactly, maybe a lifetime and a bit".

II

Part Two

11

Return to Jula Island

After speaking with Dr. Cynthia Giles and Sean Smith, we decided to meet at my office the following July at the Buchanan building at UBC. We agreed that our impending expedition would need some younger hands on the team, and we would recruit one graduate student each to come along. I decided I would approach the Department of Anthropology and speak with Dr. Switzer, who was the faculty lead in charge of the Edwards Trust. After Dr. Edwards went missing and was eventually declared deceased, the UBC Board of Governors opened a Trust Fund to honour Dr. Edwards and his contributions to anthropology field research.

Over the years, many anthropological expeditions have been partially funded by the Edwards Trust. I intended to put a proposal forward for the Jula Island Expedition. I reviewed the funding requirements and found that allowable costs include travel, lodging and per diem, minor equipment, supplies, and student and temporary help costs associated with the expedition. The journey to and from northern Vancouver Island has vastly improved since 1976; a 90-minute ferry and a scenic 5-hour drive will get all of us to Port Hardy. From there, a charter boat takes 5 miles to Jula Island just outside Blunden Harbour. Over the years, the Lee Lake area has been actively logged; there are numerous active and deactivated logging sites in the immediate vicinity.

Our other option was to fly from YVR South Terminal to Port Hardy via Pacific Coast Airlines; they have daily service to Port Hardy most days except Saturdays. I decided our best bet was to have a home base nearest to the Lee Lake area, where Dr. Edward's notes placed him in 1976. There was a fishing lodge called Jennis Bay Marina to the southeast of the Lee Lake area, which was accessible by water taxi from Port McNeill. From Jennis Bay, we could charter a boat to take us to Creasy Bay and drop us off. From our drop-off point, we would hike the existing logging roads to Lee Lake; it was only a few miles up a rough road.

A few days later, I received a call that Dr Giles and Sean Smith were in the staff lounge at my offices in the Buchanan Building; I grabbed my notes and left the UBC archives and made my way across campus. I had been reviewing the notes, logs and pictures that had been provided by the RCMP and Campbell River SAR from the 1976 search for Dr. Edwards. I decided to bring them along and review them with Cynthia and Sean before we set out for the North Island. I met Cynthia and Sean and asked them to accompany me to the nearby boardroom. I had put out all the documents, reports and pictures related to the 1976 search for Dr. Edwards.

I decided to concentrate on the notes created by Mr John Hilton, who was the Campbell River SAR search leader. He'd led the original team that went overland from Creasy Bay to Lee Lake. We would be taking the same route, but we had the advantage of modern logging roads versus the rugged territory that Mr. Hilton and his team had to traverse. Mr. Hilton's notes stated he'd met S/Sgt Silberg at the Dickinson Island entrance and both had boarded the CGV Grenfell for their journey to Creasy Bay. He noted they moored just offshore at coordinates 50.96032 - 127.071199; there was a small rock outcropping and a sandy beach nearby. From this vantage point, they had a short hike to nearby Creasy Lake for access to fresh water during their time in the area.

We decided to make an itinerary for our return to Jula Island. I would be in charge of transportation to and from, Sean would look after accommodation and food, and finally, Cynthia would look after video equipment, recording and uploading data via portable Starlink software. Since all of us were on semester break, it was decided we'd set aside three weeks, possibly 4 weeks, for our adventure.

Budget-wise, I'd estimated our expedition would cost approximately $25, 000.00 which was kindly approved by the Dr. Edwards Foundation. After our meeting, Cynthia and Sean retired to their suites at the Gage Tower Residence on campus, and I decided to stay awhile and catch up on emails and begin making relevant bookings, etc. I placed an ad on the local UBC Press site asking for students interested in our Expedition to Jula Island. I received an unexpected response. I figured the word had gotten out that I was putting together the original Jula Island Team and was recruiting a few hearty souls for our expedition. Many students from the Department of Anthropology had signed up, along with many from Ocean Sciences.

I decided it was best to put together a short presentation and host all the applicants at one info session; this way, I could weed out those who wanted a free holiday versus those who were truly interested in Dr. Edwards's research and eventual demise. I booked the Hall A101 in the Buchanan building for the following Monday afternoon. I'd sent a cc to Cynthia and Sean for the info. I spent the rest of my evening putting together a short PowerPoint about Dr. Edwards and our planned return to Jula Island. After I'd finished, I joined Cynthia and Sean at Koerner's Pub for a pint or two and Guinness. We reminisced about Dr. Edwards and the time we spent with him as students; we all wondered what we would discover on our return.

12

The Truth

As the days turned into weeks, Dr. Edward's strength returned, and he could walk on his own and began to memorize the layout of Kequesta village. Being a tidal bay brought its challenges; the foreshore could be dangerous when the tide was out, and he had to be careful not to slip and fall on rocks. Over time, the food had become palatable, and he got used to the taste; his vision was getting clearer, and he could make out shapes and shadows both close and far away.

While sitting by the fire, the ocean was to the left, and he could make what appeared to be canoe shapes lined up along the shore. Behind them, he could make out tall, thin structures; he knew these were totem poles, he'd felt them with his own hands. The forest was lined with cedar plank homes, each side by side, with the doors facing the water. Based on the time that had passed and the conversation he'd had, Dr. Edward figured it was near the end of Sept or the first week in October.

During his recovery, Dr. Edwards met many people in the village, the most interesting was Captain Jefferson Davis Howell, who was the skipper aboard the SS Pacific. His ship collided with another ship called the S/V Orpheus over a hundred years ago. Dr. Edwards pondered the most obvious scenario he could think of: he was in a village of ghosts, and nothing else made sense. All those he met, the little girl, Dr. Hearn and Captain Davis had all likely passed away at sea. Buk'was rescued them and eventually became part of Kequesta village, a ghost village.

The next morning. Dr. Edwards awoke, he opened his eyes and could see the ceiling of his cabin; there was smoke lingering in the rafters, and he could see sunlight peaking through cracks in the woodwork. He felt much better than he did many other mornings; his back wasn't sore, and the arthritis in his hands had disappeared. As he got up from his cedar mat, he felt almost youthful. He rushed from his cabin down to the shoreline and glanced at his reflection. A whitening beard and long hair had replaced his usually clean-shaven face; his face was blackened with soot around the fire, and his clothes were hanging off him. He'd lost considerable weight, his cheeks were prominent, and his eyes appeared sunken, but aside from looking horrible, he felt great. As he turned around, a horrific sight came into focus; hundreds of souls walking about dressed in the clothes they likely died wearing. All their clothes were in tatters; from the very young to the very old, some First Nations, Europeans, Chinese and others mingling and chatting. "This has to be a nightmare," he exclaimed, " This can't be, I'm alive, I'm breathing!!". Just as Dr. Edwards was to shout again, a gentle hand reached out and touched him on the shoulder. It was a young woman dressed in what appeared to be 1920 Vaudeville clothing. She said, " Your sight has returned and you've now become part of Kequesta village". Dr. Edwards replied. " What do you mean? I'm alive and breathing," he said. She took his hand and placed it on his chest, "Feel for your heart," she said. Dr. Edwards placed his hand firmly on his chest, then on his neck and finally on his wrist. Nothing could be felt; he had truly joined the undead. "You'll be fine," she whispered, "now join the others around the fire and eat some food, many of us have been waiting for you".

Dr. Edwards sat on the sandy shore and leaned up against a dugout canoe. He contemplated what he'd just experienced and heard. He felt his neck for a pulse, but nothing. He grasped his wrist, nothing. He was truly deceased. He felt as though he was in a vampire film; he'd joined the undead but hadn't been bitten and died a horrible death. As he gazed around, he could see the little girl, Mary, who wore a blue dress and black shoes, very likely what she had on when she perished at sea.

He spotted Dr. Berens walking towards him, and he called out, " Dr. Berens, we need to have a conversation." Dr. Berens said, " Absolutely, I'm sure you have many questions, but can we eat first? I'm starved. Dr. Edwards rose from the sand and made his way over to the fire. He was joined shortly by Dr. Berens, who gave him a bowl of what appeared to be seaweed soup with chunks of fish and other things floating about. Aside from the sight of it, it smelled delicious and tasted the same. Dr. Edwards's eating display garnered a few chuckles from the group sitting at the fire. All of them knew that Dr. Edwards had passed over and was now one of them. Young Mary handed Dr. Edwards a wooden cup; its contents appeared to be a briny liquid with little bugs floating on top.

He thanked Mary and drank the water in it entirely; he thought to himself that it was as good as fresh well water. Dr. Edwards felt strangely at peace; a sense of belonging overcame him; he'd regained his sight and strength. After a good meal,

Dr. Edwards and Dr. Berens walked along the beach and sat upon a piece of driftwood. Dr. Berens spoke first, " I would guess you have a lot of questions about what this place is and how you have now become part of this village?".

Dr. Edwards thought for a moment, then asked, " Am I dead? "The other Dr. replied, " Yes, you've ceased to be a living being and have crossed over to another world". "But I feel fine, I'm breathing, walking and talking, how does a dead person do that?". " In this universe, you are no longer bound by human imperfection nor the maladies that shortened our lives". Dr. Edwards leaned towards Dr. Berens and said, " I will assume I was alive when I arrived here many weeks ago and likely succumbed to my injuries last night sometime".

Dr. Berens hesitated and then replied, " Yes, you were indeed alive when you were brought to me. I treated your injuries and the villagers looked after you until you passed over". Dr. Edwards felt uneasy; he wasn't getting a precise answer from the good Dr. Berens. He asked another question, " Does Buk'was have anything to do with being here and dying?".

Dr Beren chose his next words carefully, " Buk'was saved all of us from certain death, he brought each of us here to die peacefully, and we all became part of his village. Yes, you were found alive at your campsite, but you were dying from the infection in your leg, which had become septic. Buk'was brought you here, I treated you and made you as comfortable as I could until your body succumbed to your illness. Dr Edwards asked, " People will be looking for me, they know I was headed, they'll come find me, won't they?'

Dr. Berens broke the bad news as best he could, " No, any trace of your human existence has been erased, you have simply passed over to our reality, you will not return to your past life.

Anything with you, when you passed over, will stay with you, the clothes you were wearing, your paper journal and pencil." Dr Edwards asked, " Can I write in my journal?"

Dr. Berens replied, " Yes, but no one will see it except us. Dr. Edwards decided to go for a walk on the beach. He excused himself and walked toward the setting sun. As he walked the shoreline, he realized he was on a westward-facing peninsula with a bay on either side. He was on a saltwater inlet that was most definitely tidal; he guessed he was in one of the hundreds of inlets that made up the west coast.

When he turned around, he saw young Mary running towards him, " Wait for me !!" she exclaimed. Dr. Edwards stopped and watched Mary neatly run for the rocky edge with ease; she'd had many years to perfect her abilities. "I've been looking for you, Dr. Berens said you had crossed over and become one of us". Dr. Edwards replied," Apparently, I have, and I've decided to go for a walk to sort out my thoughts and figure out where exactly I am". Mary replied, " That's easy, I've heard Buk'was say we're in a place called Seymour Inlet in an ancient village called Kequesta. I go for walks at the time, I watch the ships go by and sometimes wave." "Do they wave back? asked Dr. Edwards", "I think so" said Mary. With hat in hand, Mary said goodbye and skipped across the rock toward the village.

13

Creasy Bay

It was a frosty and foggy mid-September 76 afternoon in Port Hardy as Dr. Smith and I waited for the Coast Guard Cutter Grenfell to arrive from Campbell River. We would be joining Mr. John Hilton and the rest of the Campbell River SAR team, along with Corporal Roland, to meet Staff Sergeant Ravenhill and his crew near the entrance of Dickson Island.

As we stood on the pier, the sound of the foghorn in the distance filled the air, its echo travelling through Johnstone Strait. Soon, we spotted the red and white colours of the Coast Guard ship Grenfell emerging from the fog and heading towards the harbour. As the captain brought the ship alongside the dock, a man appeared on the fore deck and inquired, "I am looking for Dr. Smith and Peter from the Dr. Edwards Expedition?" "Welcome to Port Hardy. I assume you are John Hilton from the Campbell River SAR team," I replied. "That I am. Why don't you grab your gear and come aboard? We have a fresh pot of coffee waiting," said John.

Dr. Smith and I made our way down the gangway and boarded the Coast Guard Cutter Grenfell for the first time.

Following us was Corporal Roland from the local RCMP, the lead investigator who would be joining us for the entire search for Dr. Edwards. After boarding, we were greeted by First Officer John Breland, who escorted us to the bridge, where we met Captain Roy Feness. Captain Feness reached out, giving us both a hearty handshake, and welcomed us aboard the cutter Grenfell. He then said, "My first officer, John Breland, will escort you to your cabins where you can make yourselves comfortable and then join us in the main mess where we have prepared some fresh coffee for you and Corporal Rowland." I thanked Captain Feness for his gracious welcome and looked forward to my accommodations and some hot coffee.

After settling in, Dr. Smith and I made our way to the main mess hall. As we walked along the passage, we noticed many pictures of the Cutter Grenfell taken in the far north near Baffin Island. After three years of service in the North, the ship was repurposed and made its home in the port of Vancouver. The main mess hall had four tables firmly fastened to the floor, each with six chairs. The tables were aqua blue, and a picture of the Cutter Grenfell was painted on each one. First Officer John Breland offered me a coffee cup, which I filled with a very fresh cup of coffee. There weren't many condiments, just powdered coffee cream or canned milk. As we sat down, the captain summoned the first officer to the bridge and returned a short time later with some rather distressing news. He had been informed that a storm from the southeast was going to cross Johnstone Strait, our route, which was a 10-mile passage through the storm.

Considering the Cutter Grenfell was a search and rescue vessel, most of us figured that she could handle anything that Mother Nature could throw at her. First Officer Breland informed us that it would be a rough crossing, but the medical officer would make seasick medication ready for those who might need it. He reminded us that the deck officers would be the only crew on the outside decks, and we were free to stay in our cabins or make ourselves comfortable in the mess. Each of our cabins had four bunks. I chose the bottom bunk on the port side and tried to make myself comfortable. Mr Hilton was on the bottom bunk on the starboard side, and two other SAR members were on the top bunks. Just as I was laying down the speaker in our cabin clicked twice, which meant there was an impending announcement to be made.

First officer John Breland made the following announcement: "Our Crossing time during calm weather would usually be about 2 hours; however, with the winds out of the southeast, our arrival at Robertson Island may take longer. Please stow your gear and visit the medical officer on Deck 3 if you require seasick medication".

I decided to visit the bridge while we were just getting underway, leaving Port Hardy. The bridge itself was a myriad of screen gauges without the ship's officers used for navigating all sorts of bad weather. Captain Feness informed me that he'd been in contact with Captain Murray aboard a Coast Guard ship, Louie M. Lauzier, and they were currently anchored just off the Southwest coast of Robertson Island. Dr. Smith had asked if the weather would hamper our efforts to make her way to Lee Lake and find Doctor Edwards. I reassured her that 90% of our search area was on land as opposed to being on the water.

While we were on the bridge, an incoming radio message was received from the Police Boat Harvison. They had arrived at Vigilance Point, and they were making their way into the

Seymour Inlet area. Based upon the weather, they would travel eastward towards Harriet Point and then turn Southeast and make their way to the McKinnon lagoon area. From there, they would travel overland to the Lee Lake area and the last known location of Dr Edwards. It was decided to make the best speed towards Robertson Island to be on station before the worst of the weather moved into Johnstone Strait.

While returning to my cabin, I heard the speaker click twice, "Attention all crew and yes to board the Cutter Grenfell, dinner will be served in the mess hall at approximately 1900 hours". While I was on my way back to my cabin, I was met by Mr Hilton. He said: "I've just been informed that once we rendezvous at Robertson Island, we will all board the Police Boat McClellan and make our way to Dove Island and set up a base camp at Creasy Bay".

While aboard the police boat Harvison, Staff Sergeant Ravenhill was deeply engrossed in studying maps and orienting himself for the upcoming overland journey toward the Lee Lake area. Ravenhill had prior experience patrolling the Seymour Inlet back in the late 1960s, a time when the federal government enforced the relocation of the Gwa'Sala people from their ancestral lands to the reserve in Port Hardy. Although he was not physically present during the events leading up to the relocation, he later witnessed the devastating aftermath. In the fall, he saw the original village completely razed to the ground by federal government Indian agents. This destructive act left the Gwa'Sala people with no option but to remain in the Port Hardy area, where they faced a shortage of housing, leading many to live aboard their boats full-time, with many dying.

The Harvison and the McClellan, two police boats commissioned by the RCMP in Sydney, British Columbia, were meticulously constructed on Vancouver Island. Measuring 41 feet in length and weighing around 10 tons each, these vessels were manned by a crew of four, led by a Staff Sergeant as the Captain, a Corporal as the first officer, and two Constables. Both boats were powered by dual Chrysler 440 Marine engines, enabling them to cruise at speeds of 8 to 10 knots, and were specifically designed for Coastal and Inland Water Patrol duties.

14

Revelations

After Mary's visit to the rocky Beach, Dr Edwards decided to return to his cabin and look around for his journal. When he entered his cabin, he could see his original clothing was on his cedar mat along with his journal and a pack of pencils.

September / October, 1976

Well, I'm alive. I have been told by others who found me that I had been semi-conscious and very sick for 3 weeks. A man named Buk'was had found me at my camp on Lee Lake; he transported me overland and by canoe to the Gwa'Sala Territory. I do not know exactly where I am, but I do know from talking to others that this Village is called Kequesta. At this point, I'm not sure whether I'm alive or dead. I feel alive, though I've been told very recently that I passed over. This is the first day that I have regained my sight and have been able to walk around the village. During my time here, I was treated by Dr. Berens and a young girl named Mary, who both looked after me. They fed me horrible food and wretched water when I was conscious. There are several hundred people in the village. I know the year is 1976, but many of the people I've met appear to have died 50 to possibly 150 years ago. I do not know how this is possible, though most of them have said that Buk'was had found every one of them at sea or on land after their ships had wrecked. I'm not sure if this is making sense. Am I living in a ghost Village? Is this happening? Am I alive? Or am I dead? In the coming days, I will investigate my surroundings, try to make sense of this reality, and journal accordingly.

Dr Edwards closed his journal and ventured out in search of Buk'was. He could usually be found around the fire pit or sitting in front of his house at the heart of the village. With my sight restored, I could now see a diverse array of people, each speaking a different language and dressed in attire that seemed to be from the time of their passing. Among them, I recognized French, Spanish, a hint of Russian, some Hawaiian or Polynesian, and, of course, the local Indigenous languages. Despite this mix, there was a serene atmosphere, devoid of conflict or discord. Everyone was occupied with tasks, and there was a palpable sense of harmony among them. In my mind, I was silently counting all the people I saw walking about 10, then 25, and I was way past 50 when I spotted Buk'was coming out of the tree line.

As I approached him, it was like he already knew what I was going to ask; he'd likely given the speech hundreds of times. He spoke first, " I suppose you have many questions to ask of me, and I am ready to answer all of them". I stammered at first, then said one utterance. " How? ". Buk'was drew a breath and began. "We are a small nation of spirits caught in an abyss of past lives, time stopped for all of us, but our spiritual essence survived. I was rescued by another Buk'was some 200 years ago after my ship, the Pass of Beacon, was driven on the rocks on the western shore of Vancouver Island. I was the ship's Bosun, I was the only survivor, and the crew, including her Captain, perished.

I was much the same as you, badly injured but alive. I was brought to the Kequesta village and eventually succumbed to my injuries. I like you still wear my original clothes, my physical appearance resembles what malaria did to me and my crewmates, we were all halfway to Davey's Locker by the time we were driven into the rocks. The answer you seek is yes, I did see the smoke of your fire and did seek you out. It was not my intention to bring you to Kequesta, but once you had injured yourself and fallen ill, I decided it was time to bring you to your final resting place. The others transported you via canoe from the old village site to our village here in Gwa'Sala territory. Dr. Beren's treated your injuries as best he could; however, he believed that you had become septic and already felt you would likely pass away soon. Those around you gave you water and food that would eventually end your life and let you join our community. Dr Edwards asks, "What about the rest? What about Dr. Berens what about Mary, and the others I have met?"

Buk'was answered, " Many of the others like you were seriously injured or sick or already dying when I came across them. It is in my nature and part of my being that I seek out those who are near death or dying." Dr Edwards asks, "Why bring us here? You could have brought them to a nearby village in hopes that their lives might have been saved. "Buk'was looked perplexed. He answered, "Would you rather have died at sea or have a life as it is with many others like yourself here in my village?"

Dr Edward spoke, "My people would have come looking for me, and they likely would have found me if you had just left me there." Buk'was replied, " Your friends, like many others over the years, have come looking for their lost ones. Your friends did come, but too much time had passed, and you would have likely succumbed to your injuries before they ever arrived. Dr Edwards decided to think about what he had just heard, bid Buk'was goodbye and returned to his cabin.

October 1976

I am not sure if I have met God or the devil himself; to be sure, I am likely dead but existing in a spiritual space in an ancient village in the Gwa'Sala Territory. It appears that most of us, or all of us that exist in this village, are now, and we'll continue to be ghosts of our former selves. The soul I met, named Buk'was, searched out those people who were likely to die or were dying and brought them back to this village. I have been told that those around me knew that I was going to join them and assisted me in passing to join their community. There are several hundred souls here, Mary, a young girl who was aboard of passenger ship and then met her end when the ship went down. Dr Beren's was a ship's doctor aboard another sailing Ship that had gone down in the Johnstone St. Many people speak Indigenous languages. I have heard people speaking Russian, German and some Hawaiian or Polynesian dialects. All those who had died or in the clothes that they died in. Many of the clothes are in tatters. For many, the only alternative is to use dead organic matter, like cedar or grass, to cover themselves. Over the coming days and weeks, I will endeavour to interview as many people as I can and put their stories and names in my journals in hopes that someday their stories and mine will be read.

15

The Team

The response to Dr. Edwards' expedition 2016 was overwhelming; Hall 101 A at the Buchanan building is quite large. When I walked through the door, I would say they're approximately 50 students, many from the Department of Archaeology, which I recognized and many others from the faculty of Ocean and World Sciences. Just as I was taking the stage, I saw Dr. Cynthia Giles and Shaw and Smith coming through the doors and took a seat at the rear of the hall. I introduced myself and began the presentation with slides from the original expedition in 1976. There were some giggles and laughter when they saw that I once was a long-haired hippie back when I was a student at UBC. I explained to them that the original expedition was to examine ancient remains that had been found on Jula Island. Dr Edwards had decided to add an extra expedition of his own to the interior around the Lee Lake area.

He had been told by some community members and elders that there used to be an ancient village on the south side of Lee Lake, which piqued Dr Edward's interest. He decided to strike out on his own to the location and eventually return to the drop-off point in approximately four days. After we had completed our initial examination of the ancient remains, we began to pack up our equipment for our return trip to Port Hardy.

Finally, on our last official day, most of our equipment had been stowed aboard the ship, and we were sitting around a fire on the shoreline waiting for Dr Edward's return. We will all be quite sure he would have an adventurous story to tell about Lee Lake. As the afternoon dragged into evening and the sun began to set, all of us began to worry that Dr Edwards had not returned as he had planned. Most of us sat up late that evening, hoping that Dr Edwards would magically appear from the forest. I apologize for being late, but this did not happen.

The following morning, all of us were up early and to take in the zodiac to shore, hoping that Dr Edwards would be sitting by the fire waiting for us to pick him up. Unfortunately, this was not the case; he was not there, and this is when we began to worry. It was decided that the ship's First Officer would walk in the general direction of Lee Lake and call out for Dr Edwards. We hoped that he would hear us calling for him and he would answer us back.

Myself and Lieutenant George, who was the first officer aboard the Coast Guard ship, decided to pack a small backpack with water, snacks, a compass and trail markers. Right after we arrived back at Julia Island, we set out in the general direction of Lee Lake, walking on a rugged path through old-growth forest and leaving timber cruising string approximately every 100 feet tied to a tree. We walked for approximately 2 hours, stopping every 20 minutes to call out for Dr Edwards. Lieutenant George estimated we had walked approximately 6 to 7 kilometres. It seemed unlikely that continuing would bring about any positive results.

While I was going through the presentation, I could see several hands going up, which was likely an indication that there were questions from those who were contemplating joining the expedition. I informed the group that I would take questions at the end, and the presentation was not long, maybe 15 minutes were left. I explained to the group that Lieutenant George eventually returned to the Coast Guard ship and informed the Captain that we had gone as far as it was safe to do so with negative results. Captain Murrey decided it was time to leave. He told Lieutenant George the contact the RCMP on Cormorant Island and to officially inform them that Dr Edwards was missing. The initial search results were negative.

As I continue the presentation, I inform them that an active search had been initiated and that search teams, which included a Campbell River Search and Rescue as well as the RCMP police boat from Bella Coola, had joined the search. The search team, led by John Hilton from Campbell River, entered the inlet and moored at Creasy Bay. From there, they went on foot overland towards the southern edge of Lee Lake in hopes of finding Dr Edwards.

Staff Sergeant Silberg and the RCMP crew entered Seymour Inlet and made their way toward McKinnon Lagoon. From there, Staff Sergeant Silberg and his crew made their way to Lee Lake, coming in from the north and eventually arriving at Lee Lake. After both teams arrived at Lee Lake, they eventually found the old abandoned village and remnants of a recent fire pit. They did not find Dr Edwards or any of his belongings anywhere near the campsite at the old village or around the lake. Dr Edwards was declared missing and eventually declared deceased in 1983.

Over the last 40 years myself Dr Cynthia Giles and Sean Smith have often wondered what happened to Dr Edwards. He was our mentor, our teacher and our friend. As fate would have it, recent events earlier this year have initiated a return to Jula Island by me, some of the original team and a few of you. The recovery of Dr Edward's Journal by kayakers in the Inside Passage brought us together to retrace Dr Edward's final journey. We hope that returning to the area and re-examining the field notes left by Doctor Edwards may give us some insight into how he met his end and where his final resting place may be. His journal revealed he was possibly taken to a village site, Kequesta.

16

The Roadtrip

The return to the North Island had been planned for the end of August. Dr Cynthia Giles had secured our transportation; it was like old times, but this time we were in a 2016 Mercedes Sprinter Van, what luxury. A week before departure, I had the honour of calling three lucky students, Chad, Shane, and Miles would accompany us in search of Dr Edwards' final resting place. Myself, Dr Cynthia and Sean Smith along with our student companions, left UBC and headed for the Horseshoe Bay Ferry terminal. Sean Smith decided to take the wheel; she hadn't driven in Vancouver for years, but was up to the challenge. She was cautious but got us to North Vancouver in relatively good time, considering the traffic over the Lions' Gate Bridge was backed up as usual, with 1 lane northbound.

Dr Giles had booked this on the 3:00 p.m. out of Horseshoe Bay aboard the new ferry, the Coastal Renaissance. She was indeed a grand ship with room for 370 cars and 1600 passengers; she was the newest class of ship to join the BC Ferry fleet in 2007. The crossing would take approximately 90 minutes. We all look forward to relaxing and watching the sunset from the open upper deck. I decided to skip the upper deck and make my way to the Seawest Lounge for some quiet time to gather my thoughts; I brought along Dr. Edwards' original notebook to keep me company. I had added some extra pages based on the info recorded in the notes, which included the research data I had found on Mary and Dr. Franklyn Berens in the historical shipping records.

Once we arrived in Departure Bay, we decided to travel northward on Highway 19, eventually stopping and booking a hotel in the town of Campbell River. I'd been to Campbell River several times, fishing with my friend Doug, who ran a part-time fishing charter service which I graciously volunteered a spare deck hand. Dr Giles had booked us into the Discovery Coast Inn across from the harbour, a whole lot of luxury compared to the 1976 expedition. We'd taken a ferry to Kelsey Bay and put up our tents on a grass area near the ferry terminal; the heavens decided to douse us with torrential rain for the entire night.

After a good night's rest, we set out northward on Highway 19. Our next stop would be Woss camp for a quick coffee break, and continue northward for approximately 3 hours towards the town of Port Hardy. Our road trip would take us through the Coastal Island range, and the weather had changed several times, from sunshine, fog, dark clouds, to torrential rain as we approached the North Island region. After 3 hours, we had passed our first town since leaving Campbell River, which was the logging town known as Port McNeil. The weather itself had turned, the visibility on the roadway was down to less than 50 ft, and it was like the clouds had dropped onto the road surface. The van's wipers could barely keep up with the heavy downpour that we endured until we saw the next sign, approximately 20 minutes later, that said Port Alice. While we were driving, I decided to read over Dr Edward's Journal, which I had brought along on the trip in hopes that it might add some closure to the team as we looked once again for Dr Edwards.

We arrived in Port Hardy at approximately three in the afternoon. Dr Giles had booked us into the Quarterdeck Inn, which had a wonderful view of Hardy Bay. After we'd done our unpacking, we decided it was time to go out for something to eat. We'd heard that Moe's Pizza was the best in town. We all jumped aboard the van and made our way towards the downtown area. I reminisced about Port Hardy with the crew. I said it was a growing town back in 1976; he had hundreds of new homes, apartments being built, and townhouse rows for employees of the Island Copper Mine. After some takeout pizza, we headed down to the harbour and familiarized ourselves with the location of the water taxi that would be taking us across to Nugent Sound and eventually Kequesta village.

I took the crew down to the dock and showed them their transportation for our trip to Kequesta village, the Ocean King Water Taxi. Chad and Shane had been on BC Ferries but not on anything smaller, and I suspected I'd best pack along a water sickness bag. The Ocean Breeze was 29 feet long; she could hold up to 12 passengers and 3000 pounds of freight. She could cruise along at a comfortable 30 knots. I informed everyone we'd be boarding her at approximately 930 am, it would take 3 hours to reach Seymour Inlet and a couple more to cruise to Kequesta Village.

17

Dr. Berens III and Mary

Life at Kequesta was mundane at best. Each soul had a routine that they followed each day. Little Mary could be found collecting seaweed along the shoreline every morning; others would be using long sticks to dig clams as the tide receded. I'd decided to spend my days learning what I could about some of my new friends and recording them in my journal. I considered Dr. Berens a close confidant, even though we were from different centuries; we shared a natural academic bond of sorts.

Nov 1976

Dr Berens was in Dorset in 1866. He was a Member of Parliament and a prominent landowner. He recounted his mother as distant. Dr. Berens was raised by a Governess along with his brothers and sisters. His early years were spent travelling between their country estate and their London home in the Mayfair District of London. His family had relatives throughout Europe; they would often sail to the Mediterranean and beyond to enjoy the warmer weather it had to offer.

Dr. Berens loved being at sea; he had taken an interest in joining the Navy Service someday, but his father had decided the medical profession was a sounder choice. He entered Cambridge University in 1886 and apprenticed under Dr. Archibald Clark, a cousin of his father. After 4 years of study, he officially joined the medical staff of St Thomas' Hospital in London. After 2 years of residency, he took his Surgeons Exam and was fully qualified to join His Majesty's Naval Service as a Ship's Surgeon.

Dr. Berens was looking for high-seas adventure, and he decided to accept a post aboard the HMS Oceanic, a science ship bound for the southern seas near Australia. As a Surgeon-Lieutenant, he enjoyed the company of Officers most of the time, but eventually met most of the crew either through casual contact or medical ailments he'd treated over time. In 1898, Dr Berens jumped at the chance to join the crew of the HMS Condor, a new Condor-class ship that was steam-powered. She was built in Sheerness Shipyards in England and would set sail for Naval Base Esquimalt on Vancouver Island.

Dr. Berens recounted HMS Condor's last voyage; they'd departed Esquimalt with 140 souls bound for Honolulu on Dec 2nd, 1901. The very next day, while passing Cape Flattery, she was caught in a strong gale, took on water and sank. All souls were lost except Dr. Berens, would would cling to a piece of ship hull and eventually be washed ashore. He would be rescued by Buk'was and nursed back to health, so he thought he would later pass away and join the Buk'was community at Kequesta.

Young Mary told me she was 14, her family was from Astoria, Washington, he father's name was John Hampton, and her mother's name was Mary. She said she lived in a big house in Astoria, she remembers he father taking her to the many canneries he owned. She recalled the horrible smell and the constant noise of the machines;

you could barely talk to each other over the noise. She was told by her mother that they would be going on a ship down the coast the San Francisco, he father had business to look after.

On the bright sunny day of the departure, the Hampton family boarded the SS Valencia. The SS Valencia was a small streamer only 100 feet in length; she did not possess a double steel hull and only cruised at 11 knots. She usually sails in sight of land and is excellent for fitting into small, shallow harbours along the west coast.

Mary said she was woken early by a crashing sound. She was thrown across her bunk with her dolly and hit the bulkhead. Her parents met the same fate but were tossed to the floor. Her father told them to dress quickly; the ship bell could be heard ringing constantly with ship officers running about the ship. Her father was told by the ship's Officer that they had run aground on a reef near the southern tip of Vancouver Island. When her family was dressed, they made for the top deck where the lifeboats were located. They were met with gale-force winds and giant waves hitting the ship and splashing over the side.

By the time Mary and her mother boarded the life raft, her father had disappeared after a great wave crashed upon the deck. The lifeboat was lowered into the rough sea, and the Ship's Officer tried in vain to drive the life raft toward shore, but to no avail. The little life raft succumbed to the giant waves and sank. Mary never saw he mother again, but little Mary clung to an upside-down life raft with her dolly and drifted out the sea. She said she awoke in Kequesta with Dr. Berens and her dolly by her side. She said Dr. Berens said she would fall asleep and wake again, and she passed over and joined the Buk'was community.

18

Return to Jula Island

I was up early on our departure day. Dr. Smith and Dr. Cynthia were next door getting our equipment readied for ocean travel. Chad, Shane and Miles were already outside by the van when we exited the Quarterdeck Inn. Most of Port Hardy Bay was socked in by fog and light rain, but this didn't seem to bother the many Eagles taking advantage of the pink salmon in the creek nearby. Our trip downtown took us to A&W for breakfast and then a quick stop at the local Save Foods for our camping food.

Our itinerary included a quick visit to the Jula Island site and then off to Kequesta Village. We intended to stay onsite for approximately 5 days, conducting mapping and analysis of the Old Village for possible grave sites. A friend of mine at UBC had lent me his newest toy, which was a portable Ground Tech GR-3 penetrating radar unit for scanning underground anomalies. Our young students would be in charge of laying out grids and marking specific sites for further archaeological examination. We drove the van onto the dock and began unloading our supplies. I was thankful we had three energetic and strong students along for the expedition. Thankfully the the tide was in, which made carrying supplies down the gangway a lot easier. All in all, loading went by quickly, we received a safety briefing from our Captain Ken, and we were off to Jula Island. Captain Ken took time to set his course but still relied on his compass, speed and watch, " I know these waters, I figure I can read my watch and compass better than any electronic screen". With that, Captain Ken popped his can of root beer and slowly powered up. We left Port Hardy behind and looked forward to time on the water.

Captain Ken began his seagoing career way back in 1971. He and his brother ran a small tug boat in Prince Rupert before buying their for coastal tug in 1976. He apprenticed under his brother John and eventually attended Camosun College and successfully obtained his 350-ton Tugs Master's Certificate. For the next few years, he worked on large tugs towing log booms and barges up and down Johnstone Straight. He would eventually move his family to Vancouver and further obtain his Marine Piloting License. He worked primarily out of the Port of Vancouver. After 30 years of Coastal Piloting, Captain Ken and his wife decided that Vancouver Island would be their next move. Captain Ken took a job running whale watching tourist boats out of the Port of Victoria.

He was a people person and loved sharing his adventures with his guests. Captain Ken had always wanted to return to the North Island; he and his wife decided to settle in Port Hardy. Captain Ken accepted a job working with the local First Nations, running the Ocean Breeze Charters.

After we passed the Masterman Islands, Captain Ken told us to hang on, he applied full power to the engines, and we were off like a rocket. He said we should arrive at Jula Island in about an hour, the seas were calm, and no unexpected weather had been reported. After about 15 minutes, we broke through the fog bank, and the entire west coast just opened in front of our eyes; we could see the entirety of the snow-capped west coast range.

After some discussion, the team decided we would limit our time on Jula Island given the extended time needed to get to Seymour Inlet. As we approached Jula Island, memories came flooding back to those of us who we here some 40 years ago; the trees on the island had grown to towering heights, our old camping landing was not recognizable with all the brush now covering it. Captain Ken slowly brought us into shore. He had to anchor about 10 feet out, he said we likely get our feet wet, but he dared not get closer.

The team grabbed their day packs, and I grabbed mine along with Dr. Edwards' Journal as we made our way ashore. After some searching, we found out original campsite, a few stands of twine were still visible tied to now mature trees, we cleared a small area and broke out some coffee and bagels. Dr Giles told the new group that when we were their age, when we last stepped on Jula Island, we'd joined Dr. Edwards' expedition to examine ancient remains. Some years later, the remains of the two girls were returned to the Nakwaxda'xw Nation and reburied on the Island in an unknown location. As I was sitting there, I felt a cold breeze brush past me. It was so cold I shivered and clenched my teeth. It was an odd feeling since no one else seemed to feel the breeze that swept across the old campsite. We spent the short time on Jula Island reminiscing about our first expedition, the friends we made and the fateful loss of Dr. Edwards. Before long, Captain Ken was calling to us to board the Ocean Breeze; we were losing our favourable tide, and he didn't want to be stuck in the shallows. With that, we all jumped aboard for a long trip to Seymour Inlet. It was much longer for others on board; good thing I brought along a few extra bags.

19

Kequesta Village

After we left Jula Island, we made our way past Robinson Island and into the Johnstone Straight; as we turned north, we encountered growing swells as we picked up speed toward Seymour Inlet. In less than an hour, Mother Nature turned her anger upon the Ocean Breeze. We were being tossed about like a cork; Shane and Miles both clung to their little white bag and expelled much of their lunch as we progressed.

Captain Ken decided it would be safer to seek a sheltered cove to wait out the impending storm. Captain Ken made a hard turn to starboard. He clung close to the coast and made his way at best speed to March Bay. He knew there was a manned fish farm operating in the area. After 20 minutes of being tossed around, the sea calmed as we approached Marsh Bay. Captain Ken had radioed ahead, and there was a welcoming committee on the barge deck.

I heard of fish farms but had never been to one. The barge bunk house, warehouse and house were at least 100 feet long, and the net pens extended hundreds of feet into Marsh Bay. We were welcomed the Jimmy Harrison, who was the crew manager. He introduced us the Barney and Peter as we made our way inside. Jimmy said, "You picked a hell of a day for a cruise, your crew looks a little green". Captain Ken replied, " We were on our way to Seymour when the storm decided to turn the straight into a roller coaster". Jimmy said, "We have room, ya, Barney, will get everyone settled, and Pete will make us a great dinner".

The crew quarters were minimal but comfortable. Shane and Miles were going to have a long night. The barge quarters slowly rocked with the incoming waves. After a great dinner, we all settled in for an unexpected night's sleep. I was gently rocked to sleep by the wind, waves, and bird calls in the distance. We were up early in the morning, Shane and Miles managed to survive the night, both were ready to go with coffee in hand, the storm had passed, and better weather was on the horizon.

We all boarded and took our seats. Captain Ken said, " Drop the lines!" and we were off again into Johnstone straight. After an hour of cruising, we were approaching the Wallace Islands, a historic site by BC standards with an interesting past. Captain Ken said, " It was first surveyed by the Royal Navy in 1853 and named The Narrow Islands. It later changed in 1905 to the Wallace Islands in memory of Captain Wallace Houston, who had originally mapped the coast about the HMS Trimcomlee. The first official resident was Jeremiah Chivers, a Scotsman who lived on the Island from the 1890s til his passing in 1927. He was an early pioneer on Salt Spring Island, but decided to buy his island, and many of the original fruit trees he planted still flourish today." Captain Ken was an armchair historian; he loved spending his off time researching local place names and talking to locals about the colourful history. The tour continued with a short lunch break out of the wind in Southgate Island

Group; our next stop be Schooner Channel and the entrance to Seymour Inlet. Captain Ken asked, " Does anyone know a little Spanish?" Miles piped up and said, " A little to get by on Vacation". Captain Ken said, " We are headed into the Salida de las Goletas". Miles guessed, " Salida means exit, and I have no idea what the rest means". Captain Ken said, " The early Spanish explorers called their ships Goletas, which roughly translates to Schooner, and so Salida de las Goletas means Exit of the Schooners".

As the hours counted down, we would see our destination after we passed through Nakwakto Rapids at the end of Schooner Channel. Captain Ken said, " Hang on, the Nakwakto Rapids are the world's fastest flowing tidal rapids in the world". We could hear the current as it slammed headlong into a solitary rock middle of the channel; the mighty tide could wash you onto the rock in a heartbeat. As we passed the rapids, Captain Ken said, " There she is, Kequesta Village dead ahead, we'll be there in 20 minutes or so".

20

The Searchers

Dr. Edwards was always interested in passing boats and ships; over time, he began to recognize their engine noise and often waved, knowing that no one could see him. On this day, he heard a familiar sound; it was the quiet rumble of Ocean Breeze, a fast charter craft that passed by many times over the years. Something was odd this time; she was coming straight towards the village and not hugging the far shore as she normally did. Dr. Edwards alerted Dr. Berens, and he said the same, " Ignore them, they can't see us or anything else except trees and sand". I ask Captain Ken what he knew about Kequesta, and he said," Not much, it was old Gwa'Sala village, it's rumoured to be an old graveyard of sorts, I've never dropped off anyone on its shores". I pointed out to Captain Ken that the marine map said the nearby Islands were Holmes Islets. He replied, " Yes, it's a reference to people who live near islands, some old Scottish folktale I'm told".

Captain Ken chose the bay on the north side, which had intertidal shallows and a decent landing beach. Slowly, he nudged us into shore, and with that, we'd arrived at Kequesta

Village as described in Dr. Edwards' Journal. Dr. Edwards crossed the small peninsula and saw an unbelievable sight; there stood Peter, Cynthia and Sean on the sandy beach unloading gear from the Ocean Breeze.

"It couldn't be, my journal was the only reference this place, it must've been found it and returned to Peter." Dr. Edwards exited the forest and made his way towards the group, Peter, Cynthia and Sean all suddenly felt a cold chill; they looked at each other, bewildered. Dr. Berens came up behind Dr. Edwards. He said. "Do you know these people?" "Yes, they were my students in 1976," replied Dr. Edwards. Both watched as Chad, Shane and Miles unloaded a myriad of supplies, which included tents, camp stoves and scientific gear. Dr. Smith had found a flat open area just inside the tree line. She told the students to bring the gear up; she would help set up camp.

Dr. Edwards and Dr. Berens were joined by Buk'was. He was very angry, " How could this happen !! " he exclaimed, "These are not welcome visitors, more will come if we don't make this right. "How ?" said Dr.Edwards. "Buk'was hasn't shared everything with you; you've only been here a short time compared to the rest of us," said Dr. Berens. " I don't want any harm to befall them," said Dr. Edwards.

With everything ashore, Captain Ken said goodbye; he was headed to Warner Bay for a pick up and returning to Port Hardy; he would be back in 5 days. It was decided we'd all share two of the cabin tents, and there were some interior curtains to provide some privacy. Our campsite was elevated; it was approximately 10 feet above the tide line, so we'd stay dry and not have to worry about high tides. After camp was set up, we sat down for a hardy lunch of wieners, beans and campfire coffee.

I told the group we would break up into small teams, but first, Miles and I would do some timber cruising and set out the perimeter of our study area. Miles and I set out due north, towards an unknown lake we'd seen on old survey maps. The terrain was rough going, and we set out a timber tape about every 50 feet or so. When we reached the lake, we turned westward and reset our GPS. After about a 1/2 mile, we again reset our GPS and headed south.

After returning to camp, we downloaded the data into the other portable GPS units and our Iridium satellite transmitters. Chad was our technical wizard; he'd brought along portable solar panels and twin Jackery Solar packs, and we'd have enough power to hold a dance party. We set up our mapping table in the corner of my tent, we drew out grid lines and plotted the search area each team would research. Miles and Shane would run the ground radar scans; Myself, Cynthia and Sean would take the lead on excavations. Chad has brought along his newest toy, a Mine Lab Manticore XP Deus 2 Waterproof Multi-Frequency Metal Detector that could penetrate up to 16 inches underground. It was getting late, a magnificent sunset gave hope that the coming days would be insightful and bring some closure to Dr. Edwards' final journey.

21

Dr Edwards

Dr. Edwards was amazed his journal had made it back to Peter, his old UBC team of students. He mused that Peter had matured gracefully, 40 years on and still all that energy. I must have done something right; they're all doctors and have pursued their ambitions. Shane, Miles, and Chad reminded him of young Peter and Robert when they volunteered back in '76, energetic and adventurous.

Dr. Berens approached Dr Edwards and said, "He is evil, you understand that they are in mortal danger if you don't get them out of Kequesta."

"How am I to do that? They can't see me nor hear me, don't think I've tried that already" Dr. Berens asked Dr. Edwards to walk down the shoreline away from the new visitors and said, "Long before you arrived, we had few visitors except for some local Elders who visited from time to time to reminisce about the ancestors buried here.

Dr. Berens said that Buk'wus, our so-called saviour, is also a shape-shifter, being that it can become someone else. He will entice them to eat ghost food that he has made to look like fresh salmon berries or clams; they will become a version of him, and soon after perish." Dr. Edward said," Can I stop him from hurting anyone? Dr. Berens answered," You brought them here, and Buk'wus is very angry with you!" Edwards said," How can I warn them and get them to leave here? Berens said, "You likely noticed they get a chill when you pass by them. I've likely seen it once when I passed by an Elder visiting; it was as if she knew I was there and looked right at me. I brushed by her again, and she turned flush like she was very hot; it felt like she could see. Be careful, Buk'wus will be watching you!!

Dr. Edwards surmised that he could visit Peter in his tent and test Dr. Berens' theory, which was a long shot, but he had to do something before something terrible happened.

Later that same evening, Dr. Edwards visited their camp and sat just outside the circle of chairs they had set up around the fire. He was amazed by the technology that they had brought along and the scope in which they intended to search the area. Just the Buk'wus appeared through the trees and began walking toward the campfire.

He walked directly through the fire. The small fire quickly turned into a cloud of white smoke and steam, with ashes flying everywhere and embers falling on Peter, Chad, and Cynthia. It was like he'd thrown seawater on the fire. He looked directly at me and said, "Worse is yet to come; this is their warning," he yelled as he stormed back into the forest.

Miles tended to the fire while Peter, Chad and Cynthia checked themselves over for burns. Shane said, "That was quite the wind gust. Is anyone hurt?.

22

Uncovered

The morning was crisp. Miles was early, making coffee in our makeshift kitchen/dining hall, and the smell of sizzling bacon filled the camp. After everyone was up, we set out to get our gear ready for a first grid search. It was simply a walk-through, looking for anomalies or just something that was out of place in our isolated location. I reminded everyone that Kequesta was a very old 'Nakwaxda'xw village site, and there was a reasonable likelihood that we would find some artifacts.

We'd been asked by the 'Nakwaxda'xw Elders not to disturb burial sites or remnants of totem poles or plank houses. After our briefing, we all headed in a northerly direction, divided into teams of two, strolling and taking note of anything unusual. Chad's metal detector was the first to ring out. Not surprisingly, it found the remnants of a stove pipe from an old house. Further into the tree line, I saw four large cedar planks, which measured 2 feet wide by 15 feet long; they were still balanced in a collapsed cross-beam on the roof. As we walked further from the shore, the forest cover began to darken the ground beneath our feet, and we had to be careful as we navigated the terrain.

It was Miles who found the first anomaly. It was a flat, round stone measuring about 6 inches. It was likely from the intertidal zone and was covered in moss and barnacles. Cynthia and Sean also noticed numerous flat stones in their grid; they took pictures and recorded the coordinates in their journals as required. Shane and Chad had come across the same, but to the west in their grid, one in particular drew their attention. It was a rough flat stone with little moss and only a couple of barnacles. Shane noted it was not like the other stones they had discovered. Chad was diligently scanning with the metal detector when it passed over the unusual rock, and it immediately rang out with a solid tone. Chad marked the site with a small red flag and took note of the coordinates.

After a fitful day of discovery, the team returned to camp with a very similar story to tell; all had found intertidal stones in the forest. Chad reported that he scanned many metallic signatures, it was worth further investigation. I asked Chad to upload everyone's findings into the mapping software, which included GPS coordinates.

Once the data was loaded, Chad suddenly took a deep breath, "You gotta see this!!". Everyone gathered around the table and looked at the image that was displayed; it was a skull. On a site over 70 acres of dense forest and underbrush, no one could lay out such a pattern so precisely. I asked Chad to identify on the map the sites of metallic anomalies, which were approximately 10 within a small grid to the northwest. We all decided to step away from the screen and come up with ideas to explain the anomalies. Shane's first offering was an ancient civilization. I concurred that some were old, but others had very few barnacles, which indicates recent movement from the intertidal zone. Cynthia said it could be a graveyard of sorts, but it didn't answer the question about its shape and size. Sean said, "Based on my calculations, I estimate there are over 300 individual sites that make that shape".

After a fitful discussion, it was decided that we would settle down, have a decent meal, enjoy a campfire, and have a few drinks. Miles was in charge of the night's entertainment. After dinner, he'd built a fire pit, set up chairs, and brought out the Bud Light, Wine, and marshmallows. As our second sunset cast an orange glow across the sky, we enjoyed each other's company and told campfire stories.

I was seated looking through the fire toward Chad when I saw him; he was standing behind Chad, looking directly at me. It was Dr. Edwards; he hadn't aged, and he was saying something. "Leave this place," he mouthed several times before he disappeared. " Do you see that?' I muttered, Chad said, " What, you were staring at me with a weird look on your face, you OK?" I decided to deflect and made an excuse that I saw something across the water. I was relieved there were no follow-up questions. I decided to take my leave and hit my rack a little earlier than the rest. Thank goodness I have extra-strength Advil; I was hoping for a restful sleep.

After tucking myself into my sleeping bag, I tried to drift off to sleep. After a few minutes, I could see my breath, but it was a hot summer night. When I looked up, I could see condensation freezing on the tent wall above my head. Suddenly, I couldn't move or yell out. As I glanced to my left, Dr. Edwards was sitting on the bunk next to me. He looked the same as the day he left us in 1976. He reached out and touched my arm. Within seconds, I could feel a supernatural warmth envelope my entire body. Dr. Edwards began to age before my eyes; his hair thinned and turned white, deep wrinkles formed on his face, and he seemed to age 40 years right in front of me. Then he uttered, "Leave this place, Peter, leave without delay". "Are you here?" I muttered. " Yes, I am here, please find me and take me home". With that, I suddenly woke up and realized I had fallen asleep while Dr. Edwards was visiting. Both Dr. Giles and Dr. Smith would share their stories the next morning, and we all had received the same visitor.

23

The Ring and Dolly

I decided it would work best if each of us teamed up with one student and examined the site of particular interest. Dr. Cynthia and Miles would examine grid sites 2 and 2 B. Dr. Smith and Shane would examine sites 12K and 12L, and Chad and I would look after grid sites 35H and 35K. The sites were chosen because Chad's metallic readings were far above normal ground measurements for an isolated area. Chad and I set out with our pocket GPS and broke a small trail to mark an easier route. After 35 minutes, we came across an east-facing open area with a thick, mossy layer, rough soil, and shrubs. I could see the red marker sticking out beside a flat rock, which had some barnacles and was about 6 inches in an oblong shape.

Chad brought out his smaller handheld metal detector and scanned the rock area. The reading indicated metallic object(s) were under the rock. I gently pushed some of the undergrowth away and slowly lifted the rock. There was a depression, but nothing was visible except a few bugs. Chad reached across and scanned again; the beep was louder this time. I slowly pushed the topsoil aside and used my finger to feel around for anything unusual. After some effort, I felt something in my hand. I clenched it tightly and gently lifted it out of the depression.

Chad poured some water into my hand and washed away the mud and debris, and a ring slowly emerged from the debris. Both of us gasped; we both knew exactly what we were looking at. It was a UBC Faculty signet ring, usually gifted to Faculty Members for outstanding contributions to the University. I pulled out my small whisk and slowly scrubbed the ring's outer surface; the UBC motto "Tu um Est" shone through emblazoned on the top. I continued to wash the inner rim of the ring, looking for the owner's inscription; there was a small inscription I couldn't read. I handed the ring to Chad to decipher the writing.

Chad held the ring at various angles and finally made out the initials C.E. 70. "It could t be the only person I knew with those initials was Dr. Clarence Edwards!! Chad said, "Are you sure?" "Yes, very, Dr. Edwards used to wear it on his pointer finger rather than his pinky; we saw it all the time; he used to joke they didn't pay him much, but they gave a decent ring". We decided not to disturb the site anymore. We replaced the flat stone, said a short prayer, and began our hike back to camp.

After returning to camp, I unwrapped the ring and placed it on the table, with all eyes fixed on the ring. Chad said, "I would guess Dr. Edwards is likely buried under the rock site." Dr. Edwards had specifically mentioned this area, and it is possible that he knew where he was buried. Just then, Dr. Cynthia and Chad appeared, holding a small collection bag in their hands. Dr. Cynthia placed the bag on the table very carefully, folding back he bubble wrap to reveal a porcelain doll which they had found, Dolly.

She appeared to be a Bisque doll with a porcelain head, hands, and feet; the rest was made of sewn cloth. It was weathered, but surprisingly, it had survived against all odds. Could it be that both Dr. Edwards and Mary were buried at the same site, a few hundred yards apart? We decided to wrap up the ring and dolly it carefully, then put the container we'd brought along. We'd continue our site examinations tomorrow.

24

Rebirth

Early the next morning, Dr. Smith and Shane set out to examine the old village site. They wanted to map the site and create a digital 3D model. The site of the village remains was leeward of the small peninsula, located on higher ground and protected from the northern gales that likely passed through. Once on site, Shane set up his 3D camera at the north corner of the collapsed structure, which was composed of huge cedar slabs. Six cedar slabs were lying in a north-south direction, measuring 6 to 8 inches thick and with an overlength of 20 to 22 feet. There were remnants of six vertical poles that had held three or four large crossbeams; this house likely had multiple levels. The local Elders had instructed us not to enter the house nor move any of the slabs or poles; we could photograph at our leisure.

Dr. Smith was on the western side of the structure when she heard her scream," I've found somebody, they're alive!!!" Shane rushed over and saw a young woman lying within the structure alongside an exterior wall. She appeared to be breathing; her clothes were tattered and torn, and she had a dark complexion.

Dr. Cynthia and Smith crawled over the wall and began

administering first aid. Dr. Cynthia told Miles to return to camp and retrieve the trauma one medical bag and the O2 bottle. Chad and Shane also took off running to pick up the clamshell gurney, blankets and portable lights. After a quick cursory examination, Dr. Cynthia said, " She is very dehydrated, there are no visible injuries, we need to move her to our camp and make an emergency call to Captain Ken" Dr. Smith said," "She is young, not far out of her teenage years, her skin is dehydrated, she had a rapid heartbeat and very shallow breathing"". She was lying on a rotting cedar mat, a wooden bowl nearby, filled with what appeared to be contaminated water, with a bit of a seaweed-like substance floating on top.

Dr. Cynthia placed the 02 mask in place. Shane and Dr. Smith clipped the clamshell gurney together and put a blanket on top. Slowly and deliberately, the young woman rolled towards the middle of the house structure. The gurney was placed under her, she was rolled on top and was wrapped up with the blanket.

Shane, Miles, Chad and I picked her up, stepped over the collapsed wall and made our way towards camp. Dr. Smith had run ahead to call Captain Ken on the satellite to request an emergency evacuation for the injured girl they had located. Captain Ken answered the call, " I have returned to Port Hardy for repairs. I will notify the Coast Guard rescue. Captain Ken immediately called the 42 Coast Guard Rescue Dispatch at CFB Comox and informed them that a young girl had been found in distress and needed emergency evacuation from Kequesta Village. Captain Ken provided GPS coordinates (51.097493,-127.460044) and a satellite phone contact for Dr. Cynthia onsite.

25

The Rescue

The urgent call from Captain Ken reached the 442 Rescue Ops Center, sparking immediate action. Operator Natalie Reeves swiftly input the coordinates into her computer, her fingers inputting the numbers across the keyboard. The map then zoomed in, revealing the secluded area of Kequesta Village Reserve #724, nestled within the heart of the Gwa'Sala-Nakwaxda'xw Nation. She continued by taking down all the details she would need for an air rescue operation, including the patient's medical distress and current conditions. Standing nearby, Major J.C. Springle immediately dispatched one of the CH-149 crews to ready their aircraft for a rescue mission to the Seymour Inlet.

At the same time, operator Christine Holmes sent a flash dispatch to the Canadian Coast Guard Station in Port Hardy to prepare for immediate dispatch instructions to assist with 442 Rescue Operations. A radio call went out to the Coast Guard SAR Cape Sutil; she was currently on patrol near Nahwitti Bar, off the north coast of Vancouver Island. First Officer Norm Bruck received the message and passed it along to Captain

Hal George, who was on the bridge with Rescue Specialist Les More. The message stated, " 442 CP149 en route to Kequesta Village, GPS coordinates (51.097493,- 127.460044), make the best time to the location to assist with medical evacuation".

Captain George entered the coordinates into the nav system, and it estimated a 2-hour transit from Nahwitti Bar to Kequesta Village at 25 knots. First Officer Bruck immediately notified Engineer Olsen that he would be bringing up the RPM to facilitate 25 knots, and the twin Caterpillar engines sprang to life, delivering approximately 900 horsepower to their powerful propellers.

At CFB Comox, CP149 had completed her preflight and was ready to lift off with five crew aboard. The Comox Air Control tower gave her the go-ahead, and the CP 149 was on its way to Kequesta Village. Aboard CP149, the crew prepared for an aerial evacuation of the patient, while Cape Sutil would evacuate the remaining passengers by water. The radio heads crackled as Captain Johns briefed the crew in the rescue, saying, "We'll be on site at GPS coordinates (51.097493,-127.460044) in approximately 90 minutes, Rescue Specialist Cpl. Lamond and Cpl. Briscoe will rappel down with a rescue basket, and CP149 will stay on station until the patient is evacuated successfully".

Back at Kequesta Village, Shane, Chad, Miles, and I lifted the gurney above our shoulders while we stepped over the collapsed outer wall. Shane and Chad led the way as Dr Cynthia and Dr. Smith monitored the patient while we made our way to camp. Once at camp, Miles cleaned off our dining table, and we placed the gurney down. Dr. Cynthia pulled out a saline solution while Dr. Smith started an IV; it was necessary to restore fluid and electrolyte balance. The young girl was dressed in a summer dress with a bathing suit underneath. She was likely a teenager and had a silver bracelet with the name Leanne engraved.

Dr. Smith noted her blood pressure was dropping dangerously low to 81 over 42, and her heart rate was 44 beats per minute. Dr. Cynthia squeezed the IV and opened the valve to allow free flow; more fluid would help bring up the patient's blood pressure. The satellite phone began ringing close by. Dr. Smith picked up the phone and pressed receive.

Rescue Specialist Cpl. Lamond identified himself, " Hello Dr. Smith, I am Cpl Lamond, I'm aboard Comox CP149 en route to your location, we are approximately an hour away, making good time. Can you give me an update on the patient? Dr. Smith replied, " She is severely dehydrated, her stats are dangerously low, we are pushing saline, she is semiconscious but far from stable. Cpl. Lamond replied, "We will be doing an airlift as there is no landing area near your location, Cpl. Briscoe will rappel down and assist with stabilizing the patient before lift. Please keep hydrated, conscious and warm. We're on route.". Dr Smith relayed the message to Dr. Cynthia, and the rest of the team was told to pack up immediately; the Coast Guard Rescue Cape Sutil would transport all team members to Port Hardy, en route from Nahwitti Bar, a little over an hour away.

26

The End

Dr. Cynthia spoke quietly to the patient, "Is your name Leanne? What happened to you? The girl replied, "Yes, I was on a fishing boat with my friends. There was a sudden flash, I felt hot air and was thrown overboard". Dr. Cynthia, " Where are the others? Leanne said," I don't know, I woke up in the forest.' With that, Leanna lost consciousness briefly, but it had answered some questions.

Not far away, Dr. Edwards was observing the goings-on. He was happy they had found the girl and was trying to help her recover. Hovering not to fall behind Dr. Edwards was Buk'wus himself; he was furious and said, "Your foolishness will cost lives before they leave here!!". Dr. Edwards knew Buk'wus was very upset that his journal had caused his village to be discovered, along with hundreds of his victims. Dr. Edwards's only hope was that the team would get away before Buk'wus acted.

Aboard the Cape Sutil, Captain George and his crew were almost halfway across the Johnston Strait. They were making excellent time, and the two Caterpillar engines were churning out over 900 horsepower. A quick radio message flashed: "Cape Sutil, Cape Sutil, this is Comox CP149, do you copy, Over." First Officer Norm Bruck answered the call, " CP149, we copy, were are approximately 55 minutes from Kequesta Village, over," "Cape Sutil, we are 15 minutes out, we are passing over Warner Bay coming in the from south east, over" "CP149, we copy, we'll meet on station, hopefully the weather hold, over'.

Shane, Miles, Chad and I packed the camp as quickly and efficiently as we could. We had to bring all our totes a couple of hundred feet to the shoreline, making repeated trips. In the distance, I could hear a helicopter coming; just then, it appeared on the horizon, following the inlet towards our location. Captain John pressed his mic," Lamond and Briscoe, make ready for deployment, let's get you on the ground, Flight Engineer Swales, be at the ready to lower the crew"".

Dr. Cynthia and Dr. Smith covered Leanne the best they could., CP149 closed the distance and began to hover directly over them. Captain John keyed his mic, "We're at 150 feet, launch team." With that, Rescue Specialist Cpl. Lamond swung out of the Helicopter in the rescue stretcher and began his journey to the ground. Engineer Olsen slowly let out the line and placed the basket approximately 30 feet from the patient. Rescue Specialist Cpl. Lamond was released with a stretcher, and he hooked back up to retrieve Rescue Specialist Briscoe.

Dr Cynthia briefed Rescue Specialist Cpl Lamond, " Her vitals are failing, her respiration has been getting shallow, her BP is stable, but her systolic pressure is not steady. Cpl. Lamond brought out the heart monitor and attached the pads; her heartbeat was weak but steady. She had not regained consciousness; Cpl Lamond asked Cpl Briscoe to begin an intibation line and begin ventilation assist for Leanne. As Cpl

Briscoe began ventilation assistance, Leanne's heart stopped. Cpl Lamond then retrieved the Life Pak defibrillator pads and attached them to Leanne. He immediately pressed the activate button, and within seconds, Leanne's body shuddered briefly. The Life Pak reset itself while looking for a sinus rhythm; none was found. The Life Pak activated again, and Leanne shuddered, then suddenly coughed and vomited.

Leanne was rolled into the recovery position while she vomited what looked like seaweed, which gave a distinct order of rotten eggs, a clear sign of hydrogen sulphide poisoning. Her following words were, "He fed me food to get me better; it tasted bad." Both Cpl Lamond and Briscoe decided Leanne must be evacuated immediately, and they would take her to Campbell River Acute Care Trauma Centre.

As they loaded Leanne onto the rescue stretcher, the distant sound of Cape Sutil could be heard powering through the Nakwakto Rapids and turning towards Kequesta Village. After a few minutes, she anchored in the channel and launched her 733 zodiac with the crew aboard. As they approached the shore, Leanne was secured to the stretcher with Cpl Lamond, Cpl Briscoe, and a crew member from the Cape Sutil handling the guidelines as the stretcher rose to the Helicopter. When the stretcher was inside the Helicopter, the line was lowered, and Cpl Briscoe was picked up. The helicopter door closed.

As the CP 149 pulled away, the team began loading totes onboard the Cape Sutil 733. Captain George radioed," Make multiple trips, we have a lot of gear to stow below". Dr. Cynthia and Dr. Smith went across with the first load; Miles, Shane, Chad, and I waited patiently for our turn. As we waited, a menacing wind and rain suddenly hit our location. We took cover as the hail started to pound us and the shoreline. Chad called out, saying he had left a piece of his equipment outside the camp and was going to run back.

When Chad reached the spot, Shane called out behind him, " Hey, wait up, I thought I would join you, less hail in the trees. With that, Shane pulled out a couple of energy bars and bottles of water from his backpack. "Hey, we have time to waste, no one's going anywhere til this storm passes over. "Thanks, Buddy, I barely ate today with all the commotion. I guess Miles and Peter are buried under one of our tarps on the beach". They both laughed.

After they finished off the energy bar and water, Chad stood up and said, "Let's get going, the weather is letting up"". Chad led, carrying his small tool pouch he'd left behind, and Shane was not far behind. As time passed, they reached the shoreline, and I spotted Chad emerging from the trees, but a strange figure stood just inside the tree line.

"Catch up, Shane!! But he did not move from the tree line. " Your time on this earth is finished," said Buk'wus. All of us then witnessed the transformation from Shane to a haunting creature of pure myth.

As Chad stood on the shoreline, a sickness took over his body. He began to wretch, and he screamed, "What's happening to me? Help!!!!!!!

Chad's horrifying transformation had begun; his hair started to fall out, his body began to rot, and his clothes fell off. The deadly stench of decay overtook those of us on the Cape Sutil; Chad's eyes, ears, nose, and mouth began to seep black fluid, and his gaping mouth could see his voiceless screams.

Chad attempted to fall into the sea, but Buk'wus leaped from the forest and jumped on what was left of Chad. Buk'wus held Chad by his head, then plunged him into the ocean. He had him under water until he ceased to struggle. Buk'wus yelled, "This fate awaits anyone who returns to my village!!" Dr. Edwards was horrified by what he saw; he knew that Buk'wus had transformed into Shane and given poor Chad ghost food, in essence turning him into a Buk'wus.

As the Cape Sutil lifted anchor, everyone stood on the stern in disbelief at what they had just witnessed, including Shane himself.

As the Cape Sutil pulled away, hundreds of people began to appear on the shoreline, including Dr. Edwards, Dr. Berens, and Mary and Buk'wus himself.

Now you know the story of Buk'wus …